MARRIAGE RUSE IN PARADISE

SUSAN MEIER

ROMANCE

Recycling programs for this product may not exist in your area.

ISBN-13: 978-1-335-47087-4

Marriage Ruse in Paradise

For questions and comments about the quality of this book, please contact us at CustomerService@Harlequin.com.

Harlequin Enterprises ULC
22 Adelaide St. West, 41st Floor
Toronto, Ontario M5H 4E3, Canada
www.Harlequin.com

HarperCollins Publishers
Macken House, 39/40 Mayor Street Upper,
Dublin 1, D01 C9W8, Ireland
www.HarperCollins.com

Printed in U.S.A.

1 2 3 4 5 6 7 8 9 10 HDC 28 27 26 25

Passport to Paradise

Final destination: happily-ever-after!

The heat is rising, adventure is calling...
So why not strap in and get swept away to
the world's most luxurious locations? Lands of
white sands, blue skies—and sizzling nights...

Follow our intrepid travellers as they check their
baggage and lose themselves in first-class romance.
But are their connections just for the summer...
or are these jet-setters en route to their
five-star forever afters?

Grab your ticket for...

Marriage Ruse in Paradise by Susan Meier

Hired for One Tuscan Summer by Jessica Gilmore

Available now!

And keep your eye on the departures board for...

Faking It for the Cameras by Justine Lewis

Surprise Reunion in Croatia by Ella Hayes

One Bed Between Rivals by Joss Wood

and more, coming soon!

Dear Reader,

This book was incredibly special for me. I loved Lilibet and Dylan. Lilibet was the embodiment of a helper. So, when billionaire businessman Dylan Olsen asks for her help, she's ready, willing and able—

Except the help he needs is a temporary wife. Taken aback, Lilibet isn't sure how to answer, but she's broke, her company is floundering and he offers the one thing she can't refuse. Financial security for a year so she has time to make her business work.

Dylan didn't expect to get such a smart, kind, wonderful person to help him convince his uncle he had moved on from his first wife's death. There's just one problem. How can they know if any of their feelings for each other are true when they are pretending to be in love? Playacting for the benefit of his uncle? Are their racing hearts and passionate kisses really part of a ruse?

Lilibet and Dylan's story is a fun, upbeat romance with underlying problems that keep them guessing and hoping, even as they're both just wounded enough to be afraid to take the next step.

You'll cheer for them. I did. I had a blast writing this story. I hope you enjoy reading it.

Susan

A onetime legal secretary and director of a charitable foundation, **Susan Meier** found her bliss when she became a full-time novelist for Harlequin. She's visited ski lodges and candy factories for "research" and works in her pajamas. But the real joy of her job is creating stories about women for women. With over eighty published novels, she's tackled issues like infertility, losing a child and becoming widowed, and worked through them with her characters.

Books by Susan Meier

Harlequin Romance

A Billion-Dollar Family

Tuscan Summer with the Billionaire
The Billionaire's Island Reunion
The Single Dad's Italian Invitation

Scandal at the Palace

His Majesty's Forbidden Fling
Off-Limits to the Rebel Prince
Claiming His Convenient Princess

The Bridal Party

It Started with a Proposal
Mother of the Bride's Second Chance
One-Night Baby with the Best Man

Fling with the Reclusive Billionaire
Secret Fling with the King

Visit the Author Profile page
at Harlequin.com for more titles.

With special thanks to Sheila Hodgson, who found me when I was lost at an RWA National conference. I never forgot her kindness that day and appreciated all her help on Lilibet and Dylan's story.

CHAPTER ONE

DEEP DOWN IN a hidden part of herself, Lilibet McDonald wished this was a date.

Sitting in The Met Dining Room on Fifth Avenue in Manhattan, she smiled at her companion, gorgeous Dylan Olsen. With his black hair and the kind of dark eyes that could see into a person's soul, he was the whole package. She'd had a sort of crush on him his final year at university, her first year. But once he'd started dating the woman he'd later married, she hadn't seen him again. Actually, she hadn't seen him in eight years. Anyone who followed Manhattan society knew he'd become wealthy, had a big, splashy wedding, lost his wife in a tragic accident and became a recluse.

So, no. This wasn't a date. It made more sense that he had an issue that needed the services of her problem-solving company, something a secretive guy would want kept from lawyers and friends. Something delicate that she could slide into almost unnoticed like pay a debt or apologize to someone he'd unwittingly offended. Something small, nothing political or criminal, just a personal thing he couldn't handle for himself. That was her business, her forte. Discretion. He'd probably heard of her work from a friend or relative, or someone they'd gone to school with, and easily found her website on the internet.

She leaned back in her chair. "I'm assuming you asked me to meet because you need help with something. Maybe for your business?"

He caught her gaze, giving her his dark, steady-eyed stare. In his blue suit and white shirt, with his black hair combed off his face, he looked as cool and sophisticated as their surroundings. One elbow on the table, his chin resting between his thumb and index finger, he studied her as if trying to figure her out.

She held herself still under his scrutiny. She should be glad this wasn't a date. He was a rich guy with a problem. If she did a good job, she could get referrals for years. Desperate for money as she was, she needed work more than a boyfriend.

"My businesses are all on solid ground, following a five-year plan that eases into a ten-year plan."

Her hope plummeted. He was like her parents. Every i dotted. Every t crossed. An overorganized planner. He wouldn't call someone for help.

Really? He'd called her.

And she'd already decided this wasn't a date.

"Girlfriend problems, then?" His wife had died

at least four years ago. Handsome guy like him would be back in the dating pool.

He snorted. "I never have trouble attracting women. And if someone wants to move on, I let them go. I guess I'm just not warm and fuzzy."

She'd give him that. After losing Janine, it wasn't inconceivable that he would shy away from long-term relationships.

"Then what's your problem?"

"My problem is something I won't discuss in the public seating area of a restaurant."

"You're not going to tell me?" She kissed what could have been a lucrative fee goodbye and saw herself going to law school and joining the family law firm as she'd promised her parents she would if she couldn't earn enough to support herself after five years. Tomorrow just happened to be that five-year anniversary. If this fee had been big enough, it might have saved her.

"Why waste your time coming here, then?"

"I wanted to size you up." He smiled briefly, taking in her long blond hair before his gaze dipped to her frilly blouse and simple beige pants. "You've remained just unspoiled enough that I think you're exactly the woman I need."

"Because your problem is…?"

"Unusual." He motioned to the waiter, and he scurried over. Dylan handed him a credit card to pay for the coffee he'd ordered before she arrived. The waiter raced away. "I thought we'd continue this out on the street where there'd be enough noise that no one really hears anyone."

"Oh, you'd be surprised what people hear."

The waiter returned with the credit card. Dylan rose. "Sometimes. But on Wednesdays the foot traffic is light. We'll be able to keep our distance from other pedestrians." He motioned to the door. "Shall we?"

She grabbed her clutch bag and led him out of the restaurant and onto Fifth Avenue.

She glanced around. Midafternoon on a Wednesday in Manhattan, people were few and far between. Just as he'd said.

"Do you know everything?"

He chuckled. "Not everything. Only the things I need to know."

"What is it that you *don't* know that makes you want to hire someone like me?"

He looked at the bright blue September sky, then back at her. "Your website said that you handle mostly personal problems."

"Yes. But nothing criminal. Simple things that people can't do for themselves for whatever reason. Like hire a second wedding planner when the first one quits two days before a wedding. Or screen nannies for a busy single mom. Things like that."

He frowned. The sun hit his gorgeous dark hair at just the right angle to make it gleam. His profile was perfect. Straight nose. Square jaw.

Tingles formed on her spine. A memory surfaced of the weeks they'd been in the same group of college friends celebrating Friday happy hour at a nearby pub. Not specific incidents but warm, happy feelings.

"My problem's a little different."

"Different?"

"It's my uncle."

She took a quick breath. "What does he need?"

"Nothing. He's a rich, grumpy bachelor, who wants me married."

Her face scrunched. The logical question popped out before she could stop it. "Why?"

"He turns seventy this year. He never got married. Never had kids. So he focuses on me. I think he thinks my wife's death traumatized me, and he doesn't want me to miss out on things because I'm afraid to remarry. I'm not afraid. I'm more aware of what I want and what I don't want, and I don't want to be married."

"Okay." She peeked at him with a new perspective. He wasn't the cocky college kid she'd met all those years ago. He was better. Experienced and confident. Which sent his attractiveness through the roof.

"For years, I've been able to ignore the fact that he owns thirty percent of my company's stock. He invested in me when no one else would. And I love him for it. But his age is beginning to make me uncomfortable. I don't want thirty percent of my company to become part of his estate, or, worse, to get into the wrong hands the way my wife's did."

She studied him, hoping something about his expression would clue her in about how his uncle owning his stock connected to wanting him to be married, or how his deceased wife's shares didn't revert to him as her husband.

His expression gave away nothing.

She said the only thing she could think of. "I understand why you'd want to keep control of your stock."

"Which is why it's a problem that he won't sell it back to me. At first, his owning thirty percent of the stock didn't matter. I owned all the rest. But when Janine died her will gave her parents everything she owned, which included half of seventy percent of my company."

Her eyebrows rose. It was curious that his wife's will gave her share of stock in his company to her parents, not to him.

"They now own thirty-five percent of the stock in my company. Just as I do. My uncle's thirty percent tips the balance. I've asked him to sell it back at least once a year, offered him double what it's worth. His response? Get married, then we'll talk." His gaze drifted over to hers. "I'm not getting married for real again."

Seeing the seriousness in his eyes, she believed him. His wife's death must have been very hard on him. She suddenly saw why he'd called her.

"You want to set something up to make it look like you're married?"

"No. I can't pretend. I actually have to be married. My uncle is sly. He'll check into it. And I plan to make it easy for him. I'll have a wedding in a Vegas chapel and send him a few pictures where at least one will have the name of the venue. All it will take is one quick phone call for him to confirm I got married."

"Okay. If I'm hearing correctly, you're saying you need an in-name-only marriage?"

"Yes. Real and legit. But it doesn't need to last long. There'll be no community property. No divorce settlement."

"So, find a woman and strike a deal."

He sighed. "Two things. Number one, as soon as my uncle hears I'm married, I will remind him that he promised to sell back his stock and I'm sure he'll keep his word."

"Sounds like you have it all figured out. What do you need me for?"

"That's thing number two. I was thinking you should be the wife."

She stopped walking and gaped at him. A million inappropriate images poured into her brain. Sleeping together. Waking up together. Laughing. Candlelight dinners. "Wh-wh-what?"

"You should marry me. Your website says you solve problems. And as you just pointed out, the fix for me is to get married. What I need is for you to marry me."

Her wishful brain was immediately onboard. He was tall, sexy, gorgeous—

But he wasn't asking for a real relationship. He wanted an in-name-only marriage…temporary. Short-term. No sleeping together. No candlelight dinners.

She shook her head to clear it. "That's not how this works. I tell you what to do and you do it. I suggested *you find* a wife. I could even help you find someone. But I don't do the thing."

"You just said you sifted through nannies and hired a new wedding planner for other customers. That's doing the thing."

She frowned. "Those were different."

"Different or not, you still did the thing."

She sighed.

"I'll pay you fifty thousand dollars a month for every month that we're married."

Her ankles buckled and almost tripped her. Fifty thousand a month seemed too good to be true. "Every *month* we're married? I thought you said this wouldn't last long."

Dylan Olsen took it as a good sign that she was no longer balking about the marriage, just about the length of said marriage. Though a bit of a free spirit, Lilibet McDonald was a pretty blonde with a sexy smile and a perfect figure. Exactly the kind of woman his uncle would expect him to marry.

She fit the bill. There was no reason to look any further.

"First, we have to convince my uncle we are legitimate. Even after he checks up on the Vegas wedding, he'll want to make sure that we're genuine. And that we're happy. Having known each other in the past, it's believable that you and I met again at a party or something and hit it off. Once he's onboard, I'll ask him to sell back the stock. Then there should be time—a few months—before we break up just so it doesn't look like I only got married to get the stock back."

"But you *are* getting married to get your stock back."

Her blue-gray eyes had filled with confusion. But she still hadn't said no.

"It can't look that way. The marriage must appear legitimate. He has to think I'm happy, settled. Not damaged anymore."

"That's a big ask. How are you going to fool someone for *months*?"

"Here's the thing. I live in Belize. My uncle lives in Manhattan. Usually, I come to New York for holidays. Those are the only times that you and I would have to put in an appearance together—Thanksgiving and Christmas."

"We wouldn't live together?"

"No!" He dismissed the possibility with the

tone of his voice. "Actually, I don't think we'll be spending much time together at all. We might have to be together the first week…you know… I'd call him and tell him we were married and invite him to Belize for a visit to meet you. But once he returns home, you could go back to New York, and we wouldn't see each other again until I came north for Thanksgiving. You'd come with me to dinner, and I'd drive you home. And we wouldn't have to see each other again until Christmas."

"So, this is sort of a one-week job with two dinner dates?"

"Yes. And my house in Belize is gorgeous. You could look at our week there as a vacation." He smiled at her. "I'll bet it's been a while since you had a nice, quiet week at the beach."

Longing replaced the confusion in her eyes. "And in that time, you would rebuy your stock?"

"Yes."

"We'd be married for a week in Belize and the holidays?"

"And the time in between—though we wouldn't see each other."

"Which is why this is going to be for a few months, not just this month?"

"The holidays lend validity to the whole thing. By then I hope to have my stock, but I still don't want him to think I duped him. He was good enough to invest in me when I needed help. I respect that and him. He can never find out I tricked him. You coming to Thanksgiving and Christmas a few months from now pulls it all together."

He could see the wheels turning in her head. It was easy money. Given that it was mid-September—still warm enough to feel like summer—by the end of the year, she'd make two hundred thousand dollars. And she needed it. A quick search had shown him that she was broke. She owned her condo but had no steady income. Right now, she didn't have enough in her bank account to pay her homeowners' association fees and her credit cards were maxed out.

Not that he wanted her desperate for money. But he needed to marry someone who wouldn't see the marriage as anything other than a transaction. Her being low on funds gave her reason to take the deal with no other expectations.

"This is a lot to process."

"It's a business deal. Nothing more. I'll give you three days to let it all sink in, then I need an answer."

"Three days?"

"The rest of today, tomorrow and Friday. Friday afternoon, my limo will arrive at your condo building. Either get in or send it away. If you send it away, no hard feelings. If you get in, Josh will drive you to my private plane. We'll meet in Vegas, have a simple wedding ceremony in the hotel chapel and fly to Belize from where we'll call my uncle." He paused and smiled. "Unless you want to stay in Vegas for a few days to see a show or gamble?"

She snorted. "Oh, honey, getting married to a stranger would be gamble enough for me."

"Not really. And I'm not a stranger. You know me. And I know you. No surprises." He took an envelope from his jacket pocket and handed it to her. "This is a simple agreement that protects both of us. I'm sorry if it feels like I'm rushing you, but, honestly, if you're going to say no, I have to move on and the clock's ticking for me."

She caught his gaze with her pretty blue eyes. "It is a lot to think about in very little time."

"I know, but you'll see that the agreement protects us both."

"Really? This isn't thick enough to be more than a page or two."

"Sometimes simple is better. This is an in-name-only marriage, with very little time spent together, and a good outcome for both of us. Don't overthink it."

With that he walked away, leaving her standing on Fifth Avenue, holding the chance for a fresh start in her right hand.

He didn't feel horrible about taking advantage of her troubles. He felt that he'd found a person who needed him as much as he needed her. *That's* what good business deals were made of.

Lilibet walked into her condo, through the foyer and into the stunning living room, as her phone buzzed with a text. The place had been her parents' graduation gift to her. She had looked at it as a leg up because she didn't have to pay rent. She hadn't factored in HOA fees, which were her big problem right now, and why Dylan Olsen's offer felt like a glass of water to a woman in a desert.

Sure enough, it was a "gentle" reminder from the condo board that her HOA fees were due the next week.

And her only source of income was Dylan Olsen.

She squeezed her eyes shut. There was no other option. She had to take the job with Dylan. She had a very small part to play. One wedding, one week and two holidays. She would look on it as an adventure, work that took her to sunny Belize. Plus, the amount he was paying her would support her for at least a year. She couldn't pass that up.

CHAPTER TWO

EXACTLY AS DYLAN had said, a limo arrived at her building on Friday afternoon. As she texted him to let him know she was indeed coming to Vegas, it whisked her to a small, private airport and she headed to Las Vegas.

Considering the drive to the airport, the flight itself and the drive to the hotel, it was seven o'clock—ten o'clock New York time—before she got to the room he had reserved for her.

She wanted a shower, dinner and to go to bed. But her phone pinged with a text from Dylan. Their wedding was scheduled for nine o'clock that night in the hotel chapel. He'd also put an outfit for her to wear in her closet.

She texted back: Great. I'll see you at the chapel.

She had time for the shower, to dress and to order room service, if she didn't waste a minute. She walked to the closet and opened the door. Her eyes bugged.

Dylan hadn't just provided an "outfit." A gorgeous white gown hung on the rack.

She pulled it out and sighed. She could not have chosen a better dress. The formfitting satin gown shimmered in the glow of a nearby lamp. Lace appliques on the shoulders were the only adornment. A bouquet of lilies and roses sat on the closet shelf.

It seemed like he'd gone the extra mile for a pretend wedding, but she understood that it had to look real for his uncle. She felt a second of guilt for fooling the poor old man, but Dylan had his reasons. After losing his first wife, he'd said he'd never get married for real again. So, technically, this was his only recourse. Plus, he'd arranged things in such a way that his uncle wouldn't know it wasn't a permanent marriage. The old guy wouldn't be hurt.

She ordered room service, gobbled her sandwich when it arrived, showered, fancied her long blond hair and slid into the dress. No matter how beautiful, the dress would have lost something if it were too big or too small, but amazingly, it fit her perfectly.

She supposed Dylan being good with numbers gave him talents beyond just business.

She grabbed the bouquet, left the hotel room and walked to the elevator, stepping inside when it arrived. An older woman in the back tapped her on the shoulder. "That's a beautiful dress."

"Thank you." Deciding she needed to slip totally into character, she added, "My fiancé picked it out."

The men in the elevator snorted. The women sighed at the romance of it. They arrived at the floor with the chapel, and she exited. Racing down the hall, she passed a happy couple, kissing as they left the little church. She congratulated them. But seeing their joy, her own wedding suddenly felt very real.

But it wasn't.

She knew it wasn't.

That was the deal.

Before she entered the chapel, she took a long breath. *This is a job. Only a job. A big job that's going to pay your bills for a year. And Dylan's reasons are legitimate. Do not overthink.*

She opened the door, surprised to discover a reception area. The fiftysomething woman manning the desk said, "Can I help you?"

"I'm getting married here in about ten minutes."

"Ah..." She turned her attention to her computer screen. "You must be Lilibet." She glanced up at her. "Lovely name."

"Thank you."

The perfectly normal conversation went a long way to settle her nerves. Then the receptionist led her to the wide double doors that opened onto the actual chapel.

And there stood Dylan, dressed in a white tux.

Her heart stuttered. Tall and lithe, with his gorgeous dark hair, he was so physically perfect that a tux made him look beyond handsome. He smiled at her and the stuttering of her heart jumped to double time.

She was about to marry this man.

Leaving the little altar, he walked toward her. "You look magnificent!"

"You have very good taste and an eye for finding things that fit."

He laughed, leaned in and kissed her cheek. Everything inside her shimmied with an odd combination of nerves and giddiness, while he seemed nothing but happy—

Because he wasn't having weird thoughts the way she was. He needed this pretend marriage. She did too. This one job provided an entire year of finances.

This—odd as it seemed—was the door to her future.

Dylan took her hand and led her to the front of the chapel where the gentleman who would officiate their wedding stood.

He bowed slightly. "Good evening. I'm Reverend Gene Strout. You may call me Gene."

Dylan said, "Good evening. We're Dylan and Lilibet."

"Take your bride's hand..." He looked at Dylan and grinned. "Oh, I see you already have it."

He did. He'd led her to the altar and hadn't dropped it. There was something so warm and so real about that that her nerves popped again. She remembered him from all those years ago, when they were young, and she'd had that sort of crush on him. He'd only been at their Friday-night-at-the-pub group four or five times, but she'd noticed him enough to remember him. Sweet, smart, funny, he was tempting. But then he'd met Janine and soon he'd fallen out of the group. Now here she was about to marry him.

The officiant began the ceremony, then asked them to face each other to repeat the standard vows. She calmed herself. She wouldn't let herself get bogged down in the past or the meaning behind the short, simple vows. In four months, they'd be getting divorced—

Though she would be faithful. She would honor the vows because she had to make this marriage look legitimate. That was the job.

"The rings?"

Dylan produced them from his jacket pocket. He gave both rings to Gene, who set one on the small podium beside him and handed one back to Dylan.

"Repeat after me. I give you this ring as a sign of my love. With all that I have, I am honored to call you my wife from this moment until forever."

Dylan slid the ring onto her finger. It was a gorgeous three-diamond, past, present and future ring. She wasn't an expert, but she knew the middle diamond had to be at least two carats—meaning the other two were one carat each.

Confused, her gaze jumped to his just as he

said, "I give you this ring as a sign of my love. With all that I have I am honored to call you my wife from this moment until forever."

The sentiment of it settled in her heart. Not mushy or overly lovey-dovey, he'd said he was honored to call her his wife. At least for the next four months. That was okay. Not a ridiculous promise. A deal.

The ring rode past her knuckle and nestled at the base of her finger, winking at her like the wave of a fairy godmother's wand.

She swallowed. Gene gave her the second ring and repeated the vows for her to say. She took Dylan's hand. Odd how different it felt to take his hand than to have him hold hers. Their gazes met again, the expensive diamond ring weighing down her finger.

She opened her mouth to say the vows, but nothing came out.

His eyebrows rose. She swallowed hard.

Four months. Four months. Four months.

Not forever.

And she would be faithful. This might be a charade. But she would live up to it. Plus, Dylan's reasons for doing this were legitimate, and he'd taken precautions so his uncle wouldn't be hurt.

She sucked in a breath and said, "I give you this ring as a sign of my love. With all that I have I am honored to call you my husband from this moment until forever."

"I now pronounce you married." Reverend Gene smiled at Dylan. "You may kiss your bride."

In that second, the full meaning of the charade hit her. Pretending they loved each other meant certain things. Most importantly, convincing his uncle. They'd have to appear to be crazy about each other and that meant kissing.

Surely she could handle kissing him a time or two?

She smiled at him. He smiled at her. Then he took her by the shoulders and brought her close to kiss her. His lips met hers and everything seemed to go sideways. The soft, gentle kiss she'd expected turned passionate right before the flash of a camera.

She pulled back, blinking at him.

He whispered, "Pictures. For my uncle."

She struggled not to say "ah." She didn't want Reverand Gene to tell Dylan's uncle that she'd seemed confused. Dylan had said his uncle would check up on things. She had to play her part.

The camera flashed again. She looked over and saw the receptionist taking pictures. Now, there was a record of her looking confused.

Great.

She slid her hand on Dylan's shoulder, stepped close and planted a passionate kiss on his lips. That would definitely negate the confused picture. But Dylan pulled her flush against him, deepening the kiss, opening his mouth over hers, twining their tongues.

She dropped her bouquet. Dear God, the man could kiss. Warmth filled her blood. Her knees weakened. Her bouquet sat on the floor by their feet.

She was vaguely aware of the continued flash of the camera, before Dylan pulled away and smiled at her.

"Happy wedding day."

She swallowed hard and whispered, "Happy wedding day."

They posed for more pictures with Reverand Gene. She worked to remove the deer-in-the-headlights expression she knew could be in her eyes. Not from the fact that she'd married someone she'd had a crush on years ago. But because she couldn't remember the last time she'd been kissed like that. Delicious warmth twinkled along her nerve endings. Her chest was tight with anticipation. It might have been a while since she'd been kissed so thoroughly, but her body knew what it meant. And it appeared to be ready. Not just physically, but like a little kid when promised candy for good behavior, it sat poised, waiting for the next step.

She was going to have to go back to her room and take a cold shower.

"We have an hour until our plane leaves."

Her head snapped around. "What?"

"You said you didn't want to stay in Vegas, so I arranged for us to fly straight to Belize. You have about twenty minutes to gather your things. I'll check us out. That way we can sleep on the plane and be refreshed by the time we get to the beach house to call my uncle."

"But I—"

He caught her gaze. Smiled. "You what?"

She could not tell him she needed a cold shower or a few minutes without him to meditate herself into zen. She couldn't tell him because her vocal cords froze, and her brain stuttered. There was no denying that he was gorgeous. Or that he kissed like someone making love. But she was a twenty-seven-year-old woman who had just entered a fake marriage as a job. She had to play her part.

She cleared her throat. "I repacked after I dressed. I only need about five minutes."

He slid his arm around her shoulders and kissed her quickly. "That's my girl."

She fake smiled. "Right."

She turned to leave but noticed Reverand Gene studying them. Which might be her fault. With the exception of that one kiss, her reactions weren't very bride-like.

"Walk me to the elevator?"

Like a smitten lover, he grinned. "Sure."

She managed a laugh though it wasn't easy. Which totally confused her. This was a job. A job. *A job.* And she'd acted in plays before. She should be acing this.

Reminding herself that this was nothing more than a deal got them out of the chapel and out of the reception area and into the hallway. Though it was fairly far from the casino floor, the sounds of slot machines drifted to them, along with the delicious scents from the restaurants.

"What did you want to talk about?"

She kept her eyes forward, zeroing in on the elevator and walking as fast as she could without looking obvious. "Nothing. I just didn't think it smart to spend too much time with Reverend Gene in case your uncle calls him to check us out. This way he remembers us kissing, not faltering over our goodbyes. Our story will hold."

"Good thinking."

When they reached the elevator, she faced him. "I'll see you under the portico in about ten minutes."

He smiled sexily. All her hormones sighed. "Aren't you changing out of the dress?"

"Yes. I'll want to rebox it to give it back to you." She'd seen the dress box on the floor of the closet. "It might be a few minutes more than ten."

"You don't have to return the dress."

Her sanity restored, she smiled professionally. "No reason to keep it."

"Maybe we can donate it?"

The elevator came. She hopped inside, all but

barring the door to prevent him from following her. "I'll investigate charities." Seeing there was a woman already in the elevator, she kept it at that.

When the doors closed, she sighed with relief.

The sixty something woman in the back of the little car laughed. "I felt the same way after my first wedding."

When Lilibet faced her, she added, "Every wedding gets easier."

"Lord, I hope not."

"Don't want to do it again?"

Having no idea who the woman was, Lilibet realized she had to get back into character as the happy, hopeful bride. "It would be nice if this marriage lasted."

"Huh. That's not the impression I got. You just gave the brush off to a really good-looking guy. Kind of hard to believe you're not racing back to your room with that one."

That was actually the problem. This relationship had all the feels for her, and it shouldn't. She hadn't seen Dylan in years. He hadn't been in their group long enough for her almost crush to become a real crush. It should have been nothing more than a footnote in her brain. Instead, her hormones rebooted the file and had fallen onboard as if it were yesterday.

"We have a flight to catch in an hour and need to grab our stuff. We dressed in separate rooms."

"How romantic."

"Yes. Romantic. That's us."

The elevator stopped. The doors opened.

The woman smiled. "You know what? I changed my mind. I have a good feeling about you. I think your marriage will last."

She scurried down the hall, probably the first bride in history to think that last line was a curse not a blessing.

Especially since she had to get through a week of living with him—with his uncle watching their every move.

CHAPTER THREE

After sleeping on the flight, they arrived in Belize so early in the morning that it felt as if the world hadn't yet awakened. A long strip of uninterrupted blue, the sky didn't have a wisp of white. The air smelled of the sea. Soft, comforting silence enveloped them like the arms of a loving grandmother.

They climbed into a sports car that awaited them, keys in the ignition.

She glanced around in awe. The country was so perfect it didn't look real. "You live here?"

He examined the area proudly and inhaled deeply. "Yes. Lucky, right?"

"Lucky doesn't even crack the top ten. I'd probably call you something more like miraculously blessed."

He laughed, maneuvering the sleek car in a semicircle that took them to a road. She sank into the luxurious seat.

He peered over. "Want the top down?"

"Let's save something for the honeymoon."

He snorted. "The house is actually about a thirty-minute drive from here." He peeked over again. Wearing sunglasses, he was even sexier than normal. "On the ocean."

"I wouldn't have expected anything less."

"That's why I said you should think of this week as a vacation."

She might have been able to do that were it not for the three big rocks on the third finger of her left hand, the lust-filled kisses for the camera and the lady in the elevator who'd said all the wrong things.

Of course, she was probably making too much of it. Stupid almost crush. She had to figure out a way to get rid of those old rushes of attraction that kept sneaking up on her. Particularly since the feelings could have nothing to do with him, but her lack of a love life. Millions of men in New York and she never seemed to meet anyone who meshed with her—even the guy she once thought she would marry had found somebody else and left her. He'd taken half her things, and she'd had to sue him to get them all back. Yet, she'd still felt lonely, missed him. Even if he hadn't loved her, she'd loved him.

"You brought a bathing suit, right?"

"Yes." Several. And sundresses and shorts. She'd looked up the weather, and she'd come prepared for a casual week...but there was something so magical about this place that she suspected she could wear blue jeans and a floppy hat, and no one would care. If she relaxed, she really could get some rest, some sun and drink some cocktails with little umbrellas.

That might really be what she needed: a week without worry about her HOA fees and her business going nowhere. Now that she had a reprieve, maybe she could plan for her future after this temporary marriage was over.

Actually, *that* was what she needed: to take her mind off the pretend marriage and onto her real-life future.

The guy driving was responsible for giving her this blessed breathing space. If she stopped focusing on those breath-stealing kisses and shifted her thoughts to enjoying a week in the sun, she could return to New York with a plan, ready to hit the ground running.

She took a breath. "You know, I didn't really sleep well on the plane. I think I'll catch a nap, so I'll be alert when we video chat with your uncle."

Dylan said, "Okay," then glanced at her. Hoping the odd looks she kept giving him were repercussions of the hectic trip to Vegas and quick wedding, he didn't push for conversation. But he had a suspicion her silence was more about those kisses. He hadn't meant to go overboard. He'd only wanted really great, passionate—*realistic*—pictures to send to his uncle. But he'd gotten carried away. She was soft and sweet and oh, so kissable...

He shook his head to clear those thoughts. Though Lilibet was gorgeous, all those years ago when he'd first met her, he'd been smitten with Janine. Interest in Lilibet had been such a quick flash that he hadn't even remembered it when he'd considered her to be his fake bride.

But he remembered now. She'd been the pretty, happy girl on the other side of the round table. Her smile had charmed him. Her laughter was contagious. But those memories had to stop. He had to get his head back in the game. He'd sent his uncle the photos taken by the chapel receptionist two minutes before he and Lilibet had gotten out of the limo and walked to the plane in Vegas. Uncle Dominic should be getting up soon to see them.

When they got to his home, they would video-call him and invite him to the beach house. Lilibet was exactly the kind of woman Uncle Dom would expect him to choose. Tall. Blond. Striking eyes. Even more striking figure. And his uncle would melt with happiness.

Unwanted attraction shuffled through him again. He ignored it because it was irrelevant. The only thing that mattered was that the optics worked. Lilibet's looks and impeccable comportment were why he'd chosen her. His uncle would expect him to marry someone tall, beautiful, poised. She was perfect, and he wouldn't spoil that with real feelings. He'd tried that once and he'd failed.

This time, the emotion that swamped him was guilt. He'd married a beautiful woman, the love of his life, then he'd all but ignored her in favor of his career. He'd realized their marriage was floundering, but he hadn't known how to fix it. So he'd worked even more.

Then Janine had been killed in an accident. He'd lost his chance to make amends. He couldn't even tell her he understood he was at fault. He'd felt like he'd fallen off a cliff. Regret and remorse had almost paralyzed him. Until he'd decided he would never hurt another person the way he had Janine. That was how he stayed sane.

Lilibet was only doing a job for him. And she would be rewarded handsomely. There would be nothing between them.

No matter how much he liked kissing her.

He passed the drive focusing his attention on the paradise around him. Forcing himself to forget the past and concentrate on the future. On changing the world. On doing something honorable to make up for his personal failings.

Lilibet passed the drive looking out the window. At first, she'd slept a bit, but she'd woken after only a few minutes. He periodically checked to see if she was nervous or bored, and when she didn't seem to be either, he kept silent. He figured if she wanted to talk, she would. But when he eased his sports car onto the driveway of his home, she came to attention.

"Your house is huge! Not just wide but tall!"

He turned off the ignition. "That's how we take advantage of the view. On the rooftop deck, you can see for miles."

She got out, staring at his shiny white house that sparkled in the sun, mostly because of the rows of huge windows and three sets of French doors that led to the first-floor patio and the decks on the second and third floors.

"Holy bananas."

He laughed. "What did you think? I lived in a hut?"

"I've been in Manhattan for so long that I forget the rest of the world doesn't have New York's space restrictions."

"So really, what amazes you is that my house is big?"

She shielded her eyes from the morning sun. "I've stayed at some big beach houses with my friends. This one tops them all."

Jeremy, a twentysomething local, who oversaw the house and grounds maintenance and sometimes filled in for the driver, walked out. "Good morning, sir."

"Good morning, Jeremy."

"I was instructed to tell you that you have a video call awaiting you."

It was still so early, that surprised him. "I do?"

"Your uncle, sir."

Oh. A call meant Dom was either extremely excited or extremely angry.

Hoping for excitement, Dylan sucked in a breath and slid his arm around Lilibet's waist. "Looks like he got the wedding pictures." He smiled at her. "Ready?"

She took a second. He swore he could see her subtly shifting gears as if going from a normal person to convenient wife. "Yes."

They walked up the sidewalk into the grand entryway with the half-circle staircase. She glanced around in awe but said nothing as they headed to his office.

His uncle's face graced the huge screen of his largest monitor. Round, but not as wrinkled as one might expect of an almost seventy-year-old, his face was all but pressed up against the camera, as if he believed he had to be right there to be seen.

"Uncle Dominic!" He let his hand leave Lilibet's waist and caught her fingers to lead her to one of the two chairs in front of the desk with five big-screen televisions that acted as monitors for his various computers. He pulled out one of the chairs. Lilibet sat on it, and he took the other.

In the little box in the corner of the screen, he could see their image and decided they looked good enough. Her in her proper slacks and lightweight sweater, with her long yellow hair billowing around her and her blue eyes sparkling, and him looking a little more beach-bum in jeans and a T-shirt.

"Don't Uncle Dominic me!" His uncle's angry bulging eyes did not enhance his appearance. "You're married?"

He slid his arm along the back of Lilibet's chair. "Hey, I thought you wanted me married."

"I didn't want you married! I wanted to go to your wedding." He shifted his eyes to Lilibet. "Is your grandma married, sweetie?"

Lilibet choked back a laugh. "Happily."

Uncle Dom leaned back. "Yeah, but I'll bet you've got a maiden aunt or two in your family tree."

"One widowed."

Dom sliced the air with his hand. "See! I could have met a widow."

Dylan blinked. "Let me get this straight. The whole reason you wanted me to get married was to troll the reception for widows?"

"I also wanted something in the newspaper. It profits me nothing to be the uncle of a genius if no one knows."

"I can get something in the paper."

"Ack." Dom batted his hand again. "What does it matter now? You've gone and done the deed."

"We have and we'd like you to come to Belize and spend some of this week with us so you can get to know Lilibet."

"So you said in your text with the pictures." He surveyed Lilibet. "She is pretty."

"And she's also here, Uncle Dom. You can talk directly to her."

"You're pretty."

Lilibet laughed. "Thank you. And we really would love for you to come down to spend time with us."

Uncle Dom sniffed. "I don't know. It's a long flight and I'm still mad at your husband."

"I get that. I remember when my sister got married. I love her and I loved that she'd found the right guy…but I was a little more interested in my new brother-in-law's frat brothers."

Dom hooted with laughter. He shifted his gaze to Dylan. "I like her."

He kissed her cheek. "I do too." His plan had fallen apart right before his eyes, and she'd rescued it. But there was still the matter of getting enough time with his uncle that he could talk about the stock. Luckily, he had a backup plan. He always did.

"How about this? I'll come up to New York next week and we can talk. I'll explain everything."

One of Dom's eyebrows rose. "Seriously? You don't think I understand why you married this gorgeous woman?" He snorted. "Come to New York whenever. I'll see you then."

As he reached out to disconnect the call, Lilibet said, "It was nice meeting you. I'll come to New York with Dylan so we can meet in person."

Uncle Dom's hand stopped midway to the computer. "I would like that."

She smiled that disarming smile of hers, and he watched his uncle melt with pleasure.

"So would I."

The old man hesitated a second but disconnected the call.

Without a word, they got up from the computer and headed out of the office. It wasn't until they were halfway up the hall before Dylan spoke.

"He likes you."

"I like him too. There's nothing like bold, unassuming honesty."

"That's Uncle Dom."

"Sorry he was angry."

He peered around to make sure no one was in hearing distance. Seeing it was clear, he said, "Are you kidding? The very fact that he was miffed is proof he believes our wedding was real." They stopped in the foyer where their luggage sat. "Wonder why Jeremy left this here?"

"Maybe he didn't know where to put it."

"You're right. We haven't told anyone yet that we're married. I guess I'll have to tell the staff." He paused, thinking things through. "You know what? It doesn't matter. My uncle isn't coming down this week. There's no reason for you to stay. You can go back to New York if you want. I'll contact you when I get there to meet with my uncle and we can plan for how to behave with him."

He grimaced. "Damn it! We don't have a story. Not only will we need to explain our quick marriage, but we need to coordinate our explanations."

"Agreed. In fact, it makes me feel better knowing there will be time to flesh out a backstory."

"So that's it. I'll see you next week sometime. Think about a good origin story for us—"

"We have an origin story. We already knew each other and ran into each other again and started dating."

He laughed. "The truth does work here."

"When in doubt, go with the truth. Then you don't have to remember a story."

He laughed again.

"What we need to figure out are the details. And they should be interesting. Or cute. Or funny. That makes everything realistic."

The foyer fell silent, and she glanced at her bags.

Picking up the cue, he said, "I'll call the pilot."

She said, "Okay," but she yawned. "Sorry."

"No. I'm sorry. I promised you a week of vacation, and I just yanked it away from you." He sucked in a breath. "I do that. I'm always analyzing, always planning, always figuring things out. Usually, to suit me. I'm sorry."

"With all that thinking, your brain must be really tired."

He snorted. "Sometimes." He combed his fingers through his hair. "Look… You took the week off—at my invitation. You should stay."

"Actually, I'm hoping to get back to New York before my family misses me."

Because she wasn't telling them about the marriage. "At least hang out for the day. Get some sleep and some sun."

She yawned again. "Yeah. Then maybe I could leave tonight."

He understood that she didn't want her family to know she'd married someone on the sly, especially since it was temporary, but if she returned tomorrow morning instead of tonight what difference would it make? Still, he didn't argue. "Leave after dinner. The chef makes the best red snapper I've ever eaten. We'll enjoy that, then put you on the plane around ten or so. You could actually sleep the whole flight home."

"Okay."

Like a good host, he showed her to the pool. Given that she was leaving that night, she left her luggage in the foyer but had rummaged through her suitcase for a bikini so she could change in the pool house.

He almost waited for her to come out. But the little floral bikini she'd carried undoubtedly left nothing to the imagination, and he wasn't one to take risks.

Their passionate kisses floated to his consciousness again, and he really, really wanted to see her in that bikini.

He told himself to get to work.

CHAPTER FOUR

DYLAN TOOK A detour through the kitchen on his way to his office. He not only instructed the chef that they'd be having red snapper for dinner; he also directed Chef Alice's sous-chef to take a fruit platter and some iced tea and water to the area with the hammock.

Later that afternoon, he sent a text to Lilibet's phone telling her that they would be eating at eight, but she could meet him on the patio at seven thirty for a drink.

He heard the door open at seven twenty-five and turned to greet her, but when he saw her, his tongue stuck to the roof of his mouth. She wore flowing white pants that fit her butt perfectly, with a pale blue halter top that brought out the color of her eyes but also showed off slim shoulders and perfect breasts.

"I hope you don't mind, but I've decided to leave in the morning."

Pleasure cruised through him. He allowed himself the moment. Since her plans to leave were now cemented for the morning, there was no risk to enjoying her company for one night. "No! That's great."

"I had to take my suitcases upstairs to get ready for dinner anyway and decided I might as well get the extra night's sleep. I took the first room I came to, by the way. Just to make things easy when I leave."

Her smile was so pretty that he barely heard what she said as it lured him over to her. Luckily, he was holding her drink. Still having trouble finding his words, he said, "Rum punch is a local favorite."

She smiled. "Thanks."

The air disappeared from his lungs, and he realized why he was so off his game. Janine had been picture-perfect pretty. Gorgeous. Stunning. Untouchable. Lilibet was a soft, feminine pretty. The kind that seduced a man before he even realized he was being enticed.

"Welcome to Belize."

They touched glasses.

"I'm going to start calling it the land of naps." She took a sip of her punch. "Oh, wow."

"I know. Best punch in the world, right?"

"It's delicious." She glanced around. "The perfect drink in the perfect place."

Most men pretended they liked women who were unimpressed with their wealth. Usually, he was one of them. But he loved that Lilibet loved his house. Not because it was ritzy and flashy and all but shouted "I have money." But because she felt good here, comfortable. From the expression on her face, he could tell she liked the same things about his home that he did.

The comfort. The relaxation. The beauty.

She set the punch on a nearby table. "I barely ate today. If I drink this whole thing, I'll fall asleep again."

He eased her hand into the crook of his elbow and headed inside. "Then let's get you dinner."

He led her to the dining room that was almost casual enough to be outside. The long wooden table had been set with two place settings. He seated her then took his place at the head of the table.

She settled herself on her chair. "I thought we'd eat outside."

"Food is meant for dining rooms."

Her eyebrows rose. "Really?"

"Stuffy parents," he explained. "Born into Manhattan society."

"Been there. My parents are highbrow lawyers. But they never confined us to a dining room at the beach." She pointed out the wall of windows facing the ocean. "Though that is a nice view."

"There are nice views everywhere in this house." Realizing how sanctimonious that sounded, he was glad when Chef Alice entered with two assistants carrying the red snapper. Lilibet smiled prettily and complimented the chef and her team as they served her.

It struck him then that he might have hired a down-on-her-luck business owner, but Lilibet had been raised in luxury herself, and she knew exactly what to say and when to say it. Still, the attraction he'd been feeling was for a woman he'd hired to pretend to like him and temporarily be married to him. Technically he was her boss.

He was paying her to be nice to him.

His stomach soured and through dinner he scolded himself for being so simple for wanting a woman he'd hired to pretend to like him.

He'd never felt so foolish.

After eating, they headed outside to the patio for an after-dinner drink, and he pulled himself together. When he went to New York, he had to convince his uncle he loved Lilibet enough for a spur-of-the-moment marriage. If nothing else, he should get to know her. Plus, they'd already recognized they needed a good story for how they'd gone from former friends to married.

As they stepped out onto the patio, Jeremy handed them two martinis, bowed and left.

"I hope you don't mind martinis."

"I love a good martini."

They tapped glasses. "To a successful marriage."

She laughed. "The woman in the elevator at

the casino told me she had a feeling our marriage would last."

Alone with her, outside where no one could hear them, he said, "Four months. In some circles that's lasting."

She laughed again and eased past the pool, over to the edge of the stone floor where she looked out at the beach.

Dylan watched her. The sound of the waves rolling to shore enveloped them. The sun had already set. Darkness somehow made it more serene.

She faced him. "This is so peaceful."

Her genuine reaction resurrected the connection he felt with her. She was sweet, pretty, sexy and he liked her for real. For *real*. He hadn't felt sincere interest in a woman in years. Would it be so bad to—

He yanked himself back from that thought. Sure, she was tempting, but they were in a temporary marriage. A business deal. She was only playing a role.

Plus, he'd been down this road before with a beautiful, wonderful woman, and their marriage had been a disaster. Then she'd died. He'd vowed he would never make that mistake again, and the only way to keep that vow was to keep his relationships with women simple. Given that they were temporarily married, even a step over the line would complicate things.

He banked any emotions he might have felt and

smiled at her. "While we have time, we could start coming up with those cute, funny details for our story."

She swirled her olive through her martini. "Don't make fun. Those details will make our story believable. You know…like our first date, our favorite restaurant, how we decided to get married so fast. Maybe you know I love lilies and chocolate covered caramels?"

"Lilies are good." He snorted. "And who doesn't like chocolate covered caramels?" He paused to actually think about their story. "If we really were married, you would know I love living here. I'm a beach guy."

She nodded and took a sip of her martini. "I love the beach too." She glanced around. "Honestly, I could live here. It won't be a stretch for me to convince your uncle that I was thrilled to move from New York." She caught his gaze. "What else?"

"The only paintings I own are Impressionist."

"I love Impressionist paintings!"

The sense that they were very much alike tumbled through him and brought back the attraction. And exchanging information? It felt like they were on a real, honest-to-goodness first date.

Which wasn't an appropriate feeling with someone you'd hired.

Hoping to break the intimacy, he pointed toward the beach. "Let's take a walk in the sand."

She slid out of her shoes and joined him as he headed to the ocean.

A few feet away from the house, he said, "Enough about likes and dislikes. Let's go straight to our pasts so we both have good background information."

She winced. "All right."

"I don't know what you're wincing about. I had a terrible marriage that was headed for divorce. Like my uncle, Janine had invested in my company when I couldn't get a bank to lend me a cent." The memory was bittersweet. Janine had believed in him. Trusted him. "I gave her thirty-five percent of my stock—half of what I owned. When she died, her will gave that to her parents."

She frowned. "You gave your *wife* stock for investing in you?"

"She wasn't my wife at the time. We were dating, not even engaged. But she wanted to invest in me, using money she'd inherited from her grandparents. When we got engaged, our prenup kept our premarriage money separate. Including that stock. Even though I'd broken through and made us both wealthy, I wanted to protect her interests in the prenup. When our marriage soured, I was glad I did. But with her parents owning thirty-five percent and Uncle Dom's thirty percent not in my control, I could lose control of my own company."

She blinked as she took in that information. "I'm sorry."

So was he. "I'm fine now. And I'm glad I kept our money separate. But all that's something a wife would know."

"Yes." She sucked in a breath as if shifting gears. "Okay. Your past is bad. But I think I'm about to top it."

The sea sloshed gently to the wet sand beside them. A soft breeze wafted around them. "I doubt it."

She laughed gaily. "My first year out of school, I was living with a guy, Ben. We met in a coffee shop and bonded over our love of bagels. It was very romantic comedy. After a week, I thought he was "the one." I mean, I was head over heels. So crazy about him I was already thinking of names for our kids, and I invited him to move in with me. About a year later, I came home one day and discovered he'd not only left me for another woman, he'd also taken half my furniture, all of my electronics and half of my household stuff like dishes as if we were married—when he hadn't bought a damn thing."

"Oh, that's bad."

She peeked at him. "I'm winning, aren't I?"

"I don't think so but let's see how your story ends."

"My parents are lawyers, and I never throw away a receipt. So I sued him. The court ruled in my favor. Not only did he have to return all my things, but also the judge tacked on a fee to pay for the moving company I had to hire to bring them back."

He studied her. She made it all sound simple and easy, but he knew it couldn't have been. "No one could think somebody was *the one*, have them unceremoniously dump them and not be hurt."

She pulled in a sharp breath, then covered it with a big smile. "Of course, I was hurt. But I got over it quickly, seeing his true colors while going through the process of getting my things back. When all was said and done, I realized that awful things like that happen all the time to people who don't have lawyers for parents, and it dawned on me that I had a marketable skill…enough knowledge of life that I could help people who were in certain kinds of trouble."

He held her gaze. That one sharp breath had given away more than she realized. There was more to the story that she wasn't telling him. Still, given that they were only temporarily married, he didn't need to pry. He just needed information about things his uncle might want to know. Her heartbreak wasn't relevant. How she made her living was. "I guess that's true."

"That's why I don't want to quit being a problem solver. I help people when they can't help themselves. It's the most rewarding thing I've ever done." She smiled with satisfaction. "I once found a band for a bar mitzvah when the group the parents had hired broke up. I found someone to drive two kids to school for a month when their mom had back-to-back weeks of out-of-town business trips and their daytime nanny couldn't drive. I also found a tutor for the son of the lead singer in a rock band, so the tutor never knew she was teaching the child of a superstar."

He laughed. "That's quite a list." It could also be how she spun her breakup to hide from the pain, but again he didn't dwell on that because it was the first time he saw the purpose of her business. He'd thought what he'd needed from her was unusual. And it was. But in general, people all over the city needed someone. And with her parents being lawyers she did have a unique perspective. Plus, she was smart and resourceful. As a businessman, he could also see that some of those jobs could net big fees.

"That's impressive."

She sniffed. "Marrying guys who need a wife isn't my only skill."

He chuckled but she suddenly deflated. "It might be impressive, but it isn't turning out to be much of a career. If I only get small jobs, I don't make enough to support myself. I need at least one big assignment a month like saving a wedding to stay solvent, and I don't always get that. Now my HOA fees are due and I'm flat broke."

"So, you didn't marry me out of pity? You needed me?" He knew that, of course, but they'd had enough serious talk. It was time to lighten the mood.

She gave him a silly smile. “Are you kidding? I married you for your good looks and charm.”

God help him. She made him laugh again and brought them back to that first date feeling. The urge to take her hand and enjoy the beach walk was so strong he almost did it by instinct. Instead, he took a step to the side, separating them a little more and brought the conversation back where it belonged.

“Let’s think about what we did the first time we went out.”

“Had dinner?”

“We didn’t also go to a show?”

“I wouldn’t set myself up for more than two hours with anyone on a first date in case there was something god-awful about you and I needed to bolt.”

He burst out laughing. “That’s brutal.”

“You’ve never ducked out on a date?”

He grimaced. “I pretend to get a text. Tell them work needs me.”

“And never call them again.”

“And never call. But in fairness, work does need me a lot. And I only weed out dates who clearly want something different than I do from a relationship.”

“And that is?”

“They usually want something serious. I do not.

I like casual flings." He paused. For as much as he wanted to keep the mood light, he wouldn't lie to her. She also needed to understand why a real marriage had been out of the question in order to appreciate how much he needed for this to work.

"Don't forget. I have a bad marriage in my past. Just when I was coming to terms with the fact that we might be headed for divorce, the woman I'd once considered the love of my life died."

The guilt of it hit him in the gut again, but he wouldn't let Lilibet feel sorry for him. No one should feel sorry for him.

"I did everything wrong in our marriage. I always put work first. And I will never put another person through that again. Ever. My dates, my relationships, are casual."

CHAPTER FIVE

He got quiet after that, barely contributing when Lilibet suggested their second date should have been at the Metropolitan Museum of Art, where they discovered their mutual love of Impressionist paintings. He said he thought it was a good idea then walked her back to the patio.

Understanding his upset, Lilibet decided not to prod anymore and excused herself to go to bed. Though he'd clearly been unsettled after explaining his failures in his marriage, she was glad he had trusted her with the story. Particularly since what happened explained why his uncle wanted him to remarry more than a desire to meet her maiden aunts.

Still, he wasn't the only one thrown off-balance. Sharing her past had brought up her own bad memories. She loved the part of the story where she could show why she'd become a professional problem solver. She hated the part where she had to admit that the man she'd loved had thrown her over for another woman—and she hadn't suspected a damn thing. She'd loved Ben with every fiber of her being and had believed he loved her too. But he hadn't and she had totally missed the signs. She'd felt like a fool. She'd *been* a fool. Which added to the pain and regret.

Ben taking her things became a diversion that she could focus on rather than how it felt to walk into an empty condo. How it felt to discover his clothes were gone. The hurt that ricocheted through her when she'd realized how blind she must have been that she hadn't noticed he didn't love her anymore.

Because years had passed, she reminded herself that she was over all that, that it had provided her with an idea for something to do with her life and therefore his leaving had been lucky. But the reminder didn't have the normal impact of feeding her spirit and bringing her out of her slump. Maybe it was because tonight the pain of it felt fresh or maybe it was because she had temporarily married someone else. Because she was free and available, she could marry a virtual stranger, and tonight she felt that hollowness in her soul.

She shook it off. She was here for a job, and she couldn't let her thoughts drift. She had to stay focused.

She walked to the room she had chosen on the second floor and went inside. Still pondering the situation with Dylan, she opened her suitcase to retrieve pajamas. The devil was always in the details of these things. Dylan might have hired her.

He might have come up with the plan to marry her. But she was the problem solver here. She was the one who had to cover his butt and make this marriage look real for at least the four months they'd discussed.

Carrying her pajamas to the bathroom where she'd showered before dinner, she stopped dead in her tracks.

She'd seen Dylan checking to see if they were alone before talking in the foyer that morning, making sure staff didn't overhear them. She'd noticed he only discussed their marriage on the patio or the beach when he was positive there was no staff around. Yet here she was sleeping in a guest room on their first night together. Spending their wedding night on a plane meant *this* was their official wedding night…and housekeeping would know they hadn't slept together. All it would take would be the right question from Dylan's uncle for someone on staff to tell him they'd slept in separate rooms. *On their wedding night.* Then she'd packed up and returned to Manhattan.

She groaned at their stupidity. After gathering her toiletries, she hunted for and found cleaning products to scrub both the shower and vanity, then she glanced at the bed, glad she hadn't yet undone the covers.

Annoyed with herself for forgetting something so basic, she texted Dylan.

Where is your room?

Third floor.

Which room on the third floor?

The entire third floor is the main suite.

She blinked at the generosity of space, then typed, I'll be up in a minute.

Why?

She decided not to answer—she'd be seeing him in a few minutes—and went in search of an elevator. No billionaire worth his salt would have an entire floor dedicated to his bedroom and not have an elevator that would take him there. She found it and used that to haul her suitcase up to his room. The doors opened onto such luxury that she paused to take it in.

White drapes blew in the breeze from the wall-sized folding doors that opened onto a deck where Dylan stood staring out at the sea. A black starburst light fixture hung like a chandelier in the center of the room. A huge California king bed sat in front of a feature wall of driftwood. Simple white linens, pillows and a comforter gave it a clean, sophisticated look. Two soft teal club chairs sat beside a fireplace that was probably never used.

For the benefit of anyone who could see the well-lit deck from the beach, she walked over to him and kissed him. The second their mouths met, she remembered the overwhelming power of their kisses at the wedding chapel, but deepened the kiss anyway. It didn't matter that her blood careened through her veins or that her body wanted to melt against him. This was a charade. It was her job to make sure it was believable.

When she pulled away, he blinked at her.

Staring into his sexy dark eyes, she whispered, "Technically, this is our wedding night."

He frowned. His eyes shifted to a mix of confusion and arousal. She wasn't sure how he would have reacted if she took advantage of his disorientation and rose to her tiptoes and kissed him again. But it didn't matter. This was a ruse. Not a real marriage or a date. Not even a shivery one-night stand. Since he wasn't keeping up with their situation, she had to explain.

Still whispering, she said, "We should be sleeping together. I should not be in a room on the floor below you." When he continued to look confused, she said, "I saw you peeking around to see if anyone was nearby before you talked about our marriage this morning. You know as well as I do that your uncle could question the staff the next time he visits. We can't leave anything to chance."

He gaped at her, his rough whisper incredulous. "So, you're going to sleep with me?"

The wonderful possibilities of sleeping with him stole her breath. She stomped them into the ground.

"Sleep," she said with emphasis. "I could probably make do with one of those club chairs. But your bed has to look slept in." She met his gaze. "By two people."

"I think you're taking this too far."

"You want to risk it with your uncle?"

He sucked in a breath, obviously thinking things through. "No, I do not want to risk things with my uncle. But you can't sleep in a club chair."

She straightened her spine, reminding herself she was the professional here and she should take charge. "We're both adults. Your bed is the size of a small country. There's plenty of space for two of us."

He glanced at the monstrosity in front of the driftwood wall. "I guess."

"I know." She grinned devilishly. "Come on. It's one night. You can trust me."

He snickered. "And you trust me?"

She waited until he looked her in the eye. He didn't want to ever get married again. He let women walk in and out of his life without emotion. He'd come right out and said every relationship in his life was casual. If she wanted that, fine. But she didn't. Plus, this was a job. A great job that paid great money. Enough to last at least a year. She couldn't screw this up.

"Yes. This does not have to be a big deal. It's what we need to do in case your uncle questions your staff."

"Okay, then."

He led the way to the bed. "Do you have a side preference?"

"Not really. I sleep on both sides, depending on the mood I'm in. So, you pick."

He said, "I sleep on the left."

"Okay. Let me use the bathroom, put on my pj's and brush my teeth. Then we need to rehearse how we're going to explain my leaving tomorrow morning when we should be on our honeymoon."

She walked into the bathroom, closing the door behind her, and Dylan cursed. He had left loose ends, but she always caught them. Now, they were shoring things up and everything would be fine. He should be impressed with how seriously she took her job—except, he now had to sleep with her.

She was gorgeous.

She was smart.

She didn't let him boss her around.

If he hadn't hired her, but they'd met accidentally that day in Manhattan, and he'd asked her out, they might be sleeping together for real tonight.

No. He had to stop thinking like that. Their situation was tricky. There could be no what-ifs or could-have-beens. He had hired her. He wanted—

no, he *needed*—to get his stock back. And she was on the ball enough that this ruse would work, if he stayed on track.

He reminded himself that his uncle wasn't coming to Belize to meet her and that all this might be overkill. But she was right about keeping the charade up for the benefit of his staff. They wouldn't look like a newly married couple if they slept in separate rooms on different floors. Though making sure the bed looked slept in by two people did feel like overkill—

He told himself to stop thinking about it.

She came out of the bathroom quickly. Her pajamas were covering from neck to ankle, but they were soft-looking, silky. Very feminine.

"Next."

He rolled his shoulders. It might not be a big deal to sleep together, but he typically didn't wear pajamas. Huffing out a sigh, he walked through the bathroom, into his closet and found a pair of sweatpants and a big T-shirt. He'd swelter, but he could turn up the air-conditioning.

When he was done and dressed, he walked into the bedroom to find Lilibet was on the left side of his bed.

"I get the left side."

She pointed beside her. "That's the left side."

"Yeah, but when you asked me, we were facing the bed, not lying in the bed. So, the left was that side."

She didn't argue, just slid over. "Good?"

The way she was so accommodating only made him feel like a grouch, so he quietly said, "Good."

As he slid under the comforter, she said, "Let's just relax and talk about the excuse we'll give for why I'm going back to New York instead of on a honeymoon."

The pillow smelled like her. He switched the bottom pillow to the top. Rather than lie down, he leaned against it. "Why can't we just say we got married spur of the moment, and you have to clean up some loose ends at home."

She pondered that. "That works." She took a breath. "But I think we're going to have to ham it up a bit about missing each other."

He shoved the pillows down and flopped onto his side. "Fine. Whatever." The angry feelings returned. He thought this was overkill and that bugged him enough he wasn't in the mood to play nice. Besides, the grumpiness hid his attraction.

She sighed. "You know…this is your charade. It benefits you if it works. But I have a reputation to uphold here. And I'm a detail person. You know how you're always thinking, analyzing, rearranging things? Well, I see details. I see when someone squints when another person is talking like they doubt what the speaker is saying. I see when someone is overly interested in something everybody else seems to be ignoring. And I'm telling you, convincing your staff is the key to making this charade work."

He flounced over to face her. "You heard my uncle. He's not coming down. I'm visiting him in New York. Plus, he only wanted me married to hit on your widowed aunts."

She gaped at him. "You bought that?"

"My uncle is weird."

"Your uncle is *worried*." She turned to her side, facing him. "Even you said you thought he didn't want you to end up alone. Your wife hasn't just died. Your marriage was in trouble. And you have a boatload of regrets. In his own way, not selling you that stock was your uncle's way of pushing you to get over that."

He huffed and rolled to his back. "Probably."

She shifted farther away from him and fluffed her pillow. "Okay. So, humor me in front of the staff. At least smile at me at breakfast. Then a kiss goodbye at the limo wouldn't be out of line."

"Fine."

"Hey, this is *your* plan. I'm just making sure it works."

She got comfortable on her pillow, the conversation apparently over. A few seconds later, he heard the soft sounds of her breathing as if she'd instantly fallen asleep. He'd never seen anybody who could sleep like she did.

But he could feel her warmth as her scent

drifted to him on the breeze that poured in from the open doors to the balcony.

He sighed. She was pretty, smart, stood up to him and smelled good.

This was torture.

He got out of bed, shut the big balcony doors and turned on the air-conditioning. He almost set it on sixty-eight, but a guy who was accustomed to sleeping nude was wearing sweatpants and a shirt. He needed the air. He cranked it down to sixty-four and snuggled into the covers. He did this sometimes to pretend he was in New York, during a snowstorm, when missing the city sneaked up on him.

The cold air and the warm blanket worked their magic and after about fifteen minutes, he also fell asleep.

He woke automatically at six o'clock the way he always did. Instead of immediately opening his eyes, he basked in the snuggly feeling of being warm in a cold room and the feeling of contentment and overwhelming happiness that filled him. He ran his hand along the slim leg that had been thrown over his, wrapped his other arm around the shoulders nestled against his chest—

His eyes sprang open. He jumped out of bed, his heart thumping, his brain going numb. He could forgive himself for the sexual effects of being pressed against a beautiful woman. That was just biology. But the snuggly feeling? The contentment? The happiness? Those were a slippery slope to a man who was done with relationships.

She mumbled, "What's wrong?"

He pointed at the bed accusingly. "We were cuddling."

She sat up. "Holy crap. I can see my breath." She gaped at him. "What did you do?"

He displayed his layers of clothes. "You forced me to wear this! Usually, the breeze from outside is enough. But I can't be under covers dressed like this without air-conditioning!"

She had the audacity to laugh. "OMG. Chill." She slid out of bed, peering around. "Speaking of chill, where's the thermostat?"

She was pretty and disheveled, so tempting that his mouth watered. He grabbed on to his anger with both hands, desperate to tamp down all the emotions pouring through him. He stormed over to the thermostat, gave it a spin as if it was a carnival game. "Seventy. Are you happy?"

She laughed again. "Oh, honey. We fell asleep. We cuddled. We survived." With that she eased by him and into the bathroom. "Get over it."

The second the door closed behind her, she leaned against it with a sigh. She'd had the most delicious dreams the night before. The past year, she'd been so obsessed with work she hadn't dated, and just the scent of Dylan was enough to send her head spinning. But being nestled against him? That was heaven.

She whipped off her pajamas as if they offended her and set the shower water to as hot as she could stand it.

She'd also had the best sleep she'd had in a long time, not three light naps a day, but an entire night's sleep. She forced herself not to ponder how long they'd been cuddled together. It was irrelevant. People could not be held accountable for sleep-cuddling. And they had a job to do this morning: convince his staff she had no choice but to leave and that they were so madly in love they would miss each other terribly.

She showered and did her hair then rummaged through the suitcase she'd left in the bathroom for suitable clothes to travel home in.

When she came out, Dylan was nowhere around. She suspected he'd found another bathroom or simply headed downstairs. After the way he'd been behaving, she would not apologize for sleep-cuddling. He'd turned down the thermostat. But more than that, it was his charade. She was only facilitating.

Not her fault.

Though her abstinence might account for her enjoying it, she was not at fault for it happening.

She found him in the dining room, still dressed in the big T-shirt and sweats, eating a bagel. His dark hair was disheveled, making him look adorable. For the benefit of anyone who might be paying attention, she walked over to his seat at the head of the table and kissed him, fighting hard against the sense of intimacy and romance that swelled through her.

When she pulled away, he looked up at her. He wasn't as confused as he had been the night before when she'd suggested they sleep together, more like sullen.

Clearly, he wasn't fighting the feelings she was.

"I left my luggage upstairs."

He blinked. "Upstairs?"

She tried to send him a message with her facial expression. *This is theater. Play your part.* Even if he wasn't happy with the charade, he had to play his part. "You know. For when the driver needs to come and get it."

"Right."

Chef Alice came in. "May I get you anything for breakfast, ma'am?"

"I would love a bagel lightly toasted with cream cheese and coffee."

She bowed. "Very good."

Dylan watched her leave, then said, "She's gone. You can talk."

"Does this room have a door?"

"No."

"Then. No. We can't talk. We'll talk when you walk me to the car."

One of the chef's assistants returned with a lightly toasted bagel, cream cheese and coffee.

As she exited, Dylan said, "What time would you like to leave?"

"ASAP." She smiled lovingly at him for the benefit of anyone who might be walking by. "If you wouldn't mind calling the pilot."

He reached for his phone. "He knows you're returning to New York. I'll just tell him you'll be at the airstrip in an hour."

"I hate to leave so soon," she purred at him, reaching out to take his hand. "I'll get that work done and be back as quickly as I can."

He gave her a funny look but sucked it up and assumed his role. "Okay."

"Will you miss me?"

Looking as if he'd eaten a live fish, he said, "Of course."

She leaned toward him and whispered. "You might want to try putting a little emotion into your voice and maybe tell your face what's going on."

He snickered and leaned toward her. Following her lead, he whispered, "Staff is accustomed to me being aloof. I think they'd be more confused if I gushed all over you."

"If you did something romantic out of character, it would actually create a lasting impression. You've gotta up your game."

So close their noses almost touched, he said, "I'm fine."

She whispered, "Not if your uncle starts asking questions."

His confusion disappeared and his eyes narrowed. "He's not even coming here."

"If he decides to check up on us because this marriage is important to him, he might call. Or maybe do a surprise visit."

He pulled back and crossed his arms on his chest. "Really?"

She nodded at his crossed arms and lowered her voice even more when she said, "That isn't helping. Get loose. Happy. You loved me enough to run away and get married. There should be some joy there."

Dylan held back a sigh, uncrossed his arms and spent the rest of breakfast, looking "loose," as she ate her bagel. But when they were at the limo and Jeremy brought her luggage to the car, he wrapped his arm around her waist and brought her to him. He would show her he knew how to play his role.

"I guess this is what happens when you have an impromptu wedding."

"Sorry. I have things I need to clear up at home."

He nodded, realizing the more she acted—made things up to benefit their story—the easier it was for him to remember to do his part.

She slid her hands up his chest to link them around his neck. "I'll miss you."

He brushed a quick kiss across her mouth. "I'll miss you, too."

Jeremy loaded her suitcase into the trunk and slammed it closed. Silent as a mouse, he turned from the car and headed into the house.

Dylan tried to step back but she held him where he was. "Don't you want to kiss me goodbye?"

He recognized that was for the benefit of anyone who might be looking then realized the driver was waiting to open the door for her. He should be better at this than he was. It shouldn't matter that he was attracted to her. This was a deal to get back thirty percent of his stock. His uncle always voted with him, but if Uncle Dom died suddenly, God only knew what would happen.

For that reason, he leaned in, drew Lilibet to him and kissed her for all he was worth. Her mouth softened under his invitingly, and he bowed her over his arm as he deepened the kiss, running his tongue along hers, enjoying her gurgle of pleasure.

Two seconds before he forgot they were acting, he eased away and whispered, "Hurry back."

She said, "After that, I'm starting to think I'm crazy to be leaving."

Her words sent adrenaline rushing to every inch of his body. But instead of reminding himself he was supposed to be acting, he reminded himself that *she* was acting. He kept falling in and out of character, but she did not. She was a professional.

With the reminder of what was at stake, he would be too.

He picked up his part. "I think you're crazy to be leaving too but I know you love your job, and I promised you we'd work out a way that you could keep it. Travel will be part of that."

Her pretty blue eyes searched his. He wondered why she wasn't saying anything and couldn't think of anything else he should say. She tapped his elbow, and he realized he still had her bent over his arm and she couldn't escape. He had to release her.

He lifted her out of his hold.

She smiled at him, gave him a quick kiss and waited for the driver to open her door.

Before entering the limo, she said, "I'll see you soon," and blew him a kiss.

He smiled and waved.

When his driver winked at him, he knew he'd done okay as a pretend lover who would be missing his new wife, and he headed into his house thanking God that she'd gone home and praying he really didn't have to see her until he flew to New York to chat with his uncle about the stock.

This was a business deal. Sleeping cuddled together had thrown him off. But he was made of stronger stuff than this. Especially when so much was at stake.

He walked into the house reminding himself

that he had never been so foolish as to be distracted from business by a pretty girl.

And he wouldn't be now.

CHAPTER SIX

LILIBET MELTED INTO the back seat of the limo. When Dylan decided to play his part, he really committed. Her entire body still vibrated from that last kiss. Again, she reminded herself that was only because it had been a while since she'd been in a juicy, breath-stealing romance, but that didn't quite hold water this time. There was something special about him, but there was also a dichotomy.

She didn't even have to wonder if he was a fabulous lover. Anybody who could set her on fire every time he kissed her knew what he was doing. Yet there was a formality about it. As if he was holding a part of himself back.

Things he'd told her about his deceased wife tiptoed into her brain. He'd explained his part in his bad marriage and wife's death and ended by admitting he was angry with himself. She could see it in his dark eyes. He'd also called Janine the love of his life. Pretending to be in love was probably difficult for him.

Would he really be able to pull this off?

She shook her head. Of course he would. He

might have nearly botched breakfast. But he'd gotten over his confusion and had played his role well at the limo. Still, she couldn't help thinking that if they spent too much time apart, they'd be starting at square one every time they were around his uncle.

They'd find out next week. She'd promised Dylan's uncle she would be with Dylan when he visited New York. The old man wasn't going to have to interrogate Dylan's staff or catch them in a slipup. If he was close enough to Dylan that he worried about him, he'd be looking at his reactions, his behavior.

And that could mean trouble.

She entered the plane, found a blanket, got comfortable on a seat and drifted off into a restless sleep. When she landed at the airstrip, a limo awaited her, along with a driver who tucked her suitcase into the trunk and retrieved it for her when they reached her condo building.

Tossing her keys onto the entryway table, she rolled her baggage into the main area of her open-floor-plan home. The farther she got, the more she was hit by the oddest sense that she didn't belong here. She blamed it on liking Dylan's beach house too much. Except she'd never really felt comfortable here.

She stopped and studied the place her parents had bought for her. The entryway led to a kitchen, dining room and a living room with a fireplace. It wasn't huge. In New York, only townhomes and luxury apartments were big. But it was roomier than most normal apartments. Still, something about the place felt awkward. Clunky. Like it belonged to someone else.

Telling herself that was silly, she shook her head. She walked her suitcase to her bedroom, plucked her laptop from the dresser and sat on the bed to bring up the email service for her website.

Nothing. No work. Not even a question.

She put the laptop away and got out her phone. She unpacked while listening to voicemails from her mom and two of her friends, hoping someone who needed help had somehow gotten her private number—though she didn't need the work immediately. Dylan was paying her enough that she could afford her homeowner's association fees and food for a year and even put some away for the lean months that always happened in her business.

Her business.

She squeezed her eyes shut. Her business didn't always pay well. She might be able to charge a wealthy father of the bride a pretty penny to save his daughter's wedding, or a rock star who desperately wanted to preserve his child's privacy, but she was more frugal with single moms or parents stuck in bad situations.

She glanced around her beautiful blue-and-white bedroom and suddenly realized why she'd had that weird sense walking into the condo. She was broke. A woman with a struggling business. Not someone who could afford this condo. The homeowner's association fees were higher than the rent on a place farther out from Manhattan.

Maybe it was hanging around with a businessman all weekend, or maybe being up against the wall had finally kicked in her problem-solver senses for herself, but she didn't belong here. She could not afford this condo.

Her trouble wasn't lack of clients. It was living beyond her means. Not because she'd planned it. Because her parents had bought her an apartment that she couldn't afford.

They hadn't done it on purpose. But their idea of making a living and her idea of making a living were two different things.

And *that* was the real issue.

This problem solver had to fix herself.

Dylan had dinner by himself that night. Afterward, he took a martini to the back pool area and stood sipping it, watching the ocean, thinking of the kiss that morning and his conversations with Lilibet. All along, she'd been smart enough to spot the million little mistakes they'd made about this temporary marriage when they were both tired and not thinking clearly. She was also warm and feminine. But she had something of an out-of-control life. Which made him curious.

He'd known what he wanted to be forever. Still,

he was a genius whose gifts guided him. What would it be like to flounder like that? To want to be something but not be able to make her business profitable?

Sympathy for her swelled in his chest. He could see she was the kind of person who wanted to help people, but being a problem solver, while gratifying enough to satisfy that need, apparently wasn't secure.

The phone in the pocket of his old cargo shorts rang. He pulled it out and saw his uncle's picture on the screen.

"Hey, Uncle Dom!"

"I changed my mind."

"About what?"

"I'm coming down for a day or two—probably a whole week. I do want to meet that bride of yours." He craned his neck, trying to look past Dylan. "Where is she?"

"In the shower." Her talk with him that morning must have stuck, because the excuse came easily. So did the realization that she might be correct. What if his uncle really was worried about him? A guy who wanted to troll for maiden aunts at a wedding reception wouldn't be craning his neck to look for Lilibet. He also wouldn't change his mind about coming to Belize. Unless he was questioning their wedding story—

He was definitely questioning their wedding

story. That's why he'd changed his mind—he was trying to catch them in their lie.

"It doesn't matter. I'll be there tomorrow to get to know this woman who persuaded you not to have a real wedding that I could go to and bask in the glow of being uncle of the groom."

Dylan laughed, not panicking because he finally felt like he was on top of the charade. "Actually, the quick wedding was my idea. But it's too late now for it to matter. I'm glad you're coming down. You're going to love Lilibet."

They talked for a few minutes, then Uncle Dom asked him to have a car at the airstrip late in the afternoon, which meant Dylan had to get Lilibet there tomorrow morning or early afternoon.

When they disconnected the call, he almost texted her to tell her, but something felt off about that. So, he hit the call button instead. She answered on the first ring.

"What's up?"

"My uncle changed his mind. He'll be here tomorrow afternoon. To meet you. To spend time with you."

"You want me to come back?"

"I'm sorry you left." He was. Not only was he curious about her, but he'd promised her time at the beach. "You should have taken the week of fun in the sun."

She chuckled. "I almost did. But I needed to

check in with my family so they don't start wondering where I've been. We're all good."

"Great." It struck him again that the answer to his problem, a temporary marriage, might not be so good for her. But she was absolutely professional about it. Including the fact that she didn't bring a laptop to their wedding. Maybe he needed to let her know that she could? After all, this was his ruse. Maybe she didn't bring her laptop to projects. Or talk to one client while working for another.

"So, repack and come down, but bring your laptop this time so you can check in with your parents while you're here."

"Okay. But before your uncle arrives, you need to figure out an entire week's worth of activities to entertain a seventy-year-old man."

"He's been here before. He likes to fish and Jet Ski, scuba dive and sit by the pool drinking martinis."

She laughed. "Is that good for his health?"

"Fishing, riding the Jet Ski and scuba diving are. And if you think he needs to lay off the martinis, you're the one who gets to tell him."

Her snort of laughter came through the phone, and he smiled. He honestly believed there was no one in his life who behaved as casually with him as she did.

"I'll send the jet. I hate to ask but if you leave at

five tomorrow morning, we'll avoid the possibility that you're both at the airstrip at the same time."

"That's okay. I can leave at five. I want this to work as much as you do."

The strangest feeling of happiness filled him. Still, it wasn't wrong to be glad she'd easily agreed to return. He had an uncle coming who definitely suspected something. He was merely glad she wasn't giving him a hard time about returning.

He stopped halfway into the house. Of course, if she was right, and his uncle was questioning the wedding because he was truly worried about him, they would have to do the best acting of their lives for the next week or so.

All the anxiety Lilibet had felt walking into her condo drifted away the next morning as she boarded Dylan's private jet. She told herself that was only because being in New York reminded her she had no work, she was living in a condo she couldn't afford and as a problem solver she should have seen that sooner. Belize had given her a day to clear her head enough to see the real problem in her life. *That* was why she was happy to be returning. She still had a lot of thinking to do.

She pulled out her laptop and did some research on rental apartments outside Manhattan during the flight but found nothing. When they landed, she deplaned, taking a long drink of tropical air, and walked to the limo Dylan had waiting for her.

She would spend these next few days on the beach, with Dylan's uncle, probably sightseeing and she would clear her head enough that she could decide her next steps.

They drove to the beach house, and she climbed out of the limo as the driver walked to the trunk to remove her suitcases.

Seeing Dylan approach, she said, "Hi."

When he reached her, he leaned down and gave her a quick kiss. For the sake of the charade, she looked up and smiled at him. Her heart filled with happiness, but she told it to settle down. They were both playing a role, and if she could be excited about anything, it should be that he was remembering to play his part.

Jeremy wheeled her two suitcases into the house and Dylan directed her to follow him. When they reached the elevator, he dismissed Jeremy, they entered with her luggage and the doors closed.

"With my uncle living with us for the next few days to a week, we have a lot of acting to do."

She pulled in a breath. "Yes. But we can take him boating, fishing, Jet Skiing, all those things you mentioned… No acting required. I'm sure we'll enjoy those outings. At least during those times, we'll just be ourselves."

"And he takes naps."

The elevator doors slid open, revealing his bedroom, and she exited. Dylan followed her, pulling her two suitcases.

"Still," Lilibet said. She glanced at the bed, remembered being curled into his warmth and stopped the feelings that wanted to bubble up. "He now has the opportunity to question the staff, so we have to be careful not to get too comfortable."

Dragging her suitcases to the bathroom, he paused and looked back at her. "Got it. And I'm good. When I walked you to the limo yesterday, I saw how much the staff is around and that they were watching. It's not just kitchen staff we have to worry about. Jeremy has two employees for the grounds. I have a driver. There are two maids. There's staff everywhere."

"This is only for a week. We can make it work."

"Thanks, but you don't need to be my cheerleader anymore. I'm good now."

"Don't think of it as cheerleading. Think of my reminders as strategy sessions."

He shook his head and continued to the bathroom, talking as he walked. "There's a closet on the other side of the bathroom with plenty of empty space. You can get yourself set up."

"Okay."

By the time she slipped out of her shoes and laid her purse on the bed, he came out of the bathroom. As he walked to the door, she headed for her luggage. Neither said another word. She would have thought that weird except their only business was pretending to be married and they'd said all they needed to.

After hanging her dresses, fancy shirts and pants, she found drawers for her shorts, jeans and T-shirts, keeping out a bathing suit and cover-up to slip into. Dylan's uncle wasn't arriving until late afternoon. She might as well have a swim and then lie in the sun to continue her soul-searching about finding a new apartment and other adjustments she might need to make to her life and her business.

Deciding Dylan was probably working, she slipped downstairs and headed to the patio with the large pool. She tossed her cover-up to a chaise, swam, dried off and stretched out on the chaise, enjoying the warm sun.

She began to think about her life, her job, her apartment, but rather than come up with ideas, she drifted off into a deep, comfortable sleep. Worried about her company the night before, she'd gone back to her normal habit of tossing and turning. But sleep came very easy on a chaise on Dylan's patio.

Sometime later, she stirred at the sound of Dylan's voice.

"Hey, sleepyhead," he called.

Lilibet shifted, but she was too comfortable and too groggy to come awake completely.

She heard his Uncle Dom say, "Don't wake her."

Dylan snorted. "This is probably her third nap today. I've never seen anyone who can nod off anywhere the way she can."

"Maybe that's good. We can talk."

Actually, they *should* talk, and alone, Lilibet decided. She turned onto her side. If she didn't fall back to sleep, she would fake it to give them the time they needed.

She heard the light noise of Dylan mixing drinks in a shaker. "Yeah. Maybe us talking is a good idea."

Now, for sure she didn't want to suddenly wake up. Not only did Dylan need to discuss his stock, but she genuinely believed his uncle was worried about him.

Uncle Dom said, "Ah. You haven't lost your touch with martinis."

"Glad you like it."

"So, I'm going to get right to it. I'm hoping you didn't get married just to get your stock back."

"Whaaat?" Dylan sputtered.

"I'm racing toward seventy and even though my parents lived into their late eighties, I know you think down the board and you worry."

"I do worry, and I do want my stock. But Lilibet is as wonderful as she is beautiful. Spend the week with us. You'll see."

"I hope."

"You know, I never really understood why you wouldn't sell me my stock unless I was married. At first, I thought it was because of Janine—your fear that I couldn't get past that—now it just feels weird."

"Not weird. I simply don't want my nephew to end up like me."

Dylan snorted. "A rich bachelor who can date anyone he wants? Your life's not a hardship."

"Actually, I'm a lonely old man, Dylan. When you get to be my age, lots of your friends will be dead or have moved to Florida, and you won't want to go out three nights a week looking for someone willing to sit and talk with you. Because that's what retirement boils down to. Being alone a lot. I keep thinking it would be nice to have someone who loved me. Someone I knew and who knew me. Someone I could travel with."

Dylan quietly said, "It's not too late."

"Oh, I know it's not too late. That's why I'm totally changing my approach and I'm actively looking for someone."

Dylan laughed. "Seriously?"

"Why does that surprise you? You had real love once. I know damn well you know what you lost, and what you missed out on."

"We were headed for divorce, Uncle Dom. I'm sort of proof positive that love doesn't last."

"Is that really what you think?"

"Yes."

"Then why'd you marry Lilibet?"

Lilibet stifled a gasp. Uncle Dom was a lot craftier than Dylan gave him credit for.

"I guess it's the optimist in me."

"Good because I'd hate to think you married her just to get your stock back."

Dylan said nothing. After a few seconds of silence, Uncle Dom said, "A toast to both of us being happy."

She heard the meeting of their martini glasses then Uncle Dom began talking about going fishing on Dylan's boat in the morning. Their conversation lasted only a few minutes before Dom said, "I think I'll take a nap before dinner."

The sliding glass door opened as the two men walked away talking. Their voices disappeared when the door closed, but she waited a few minutes before she got off the chaise lounge.

Her misgivings about duping a concerned uncle increased by ten. Not just because Dom was obviously suspicious but because he would be disappointed if he found out Dylan really had married her to get his stock back.

Two very good reasons to make sure they didn't mess this up.

CHAPTER SEVEN

AFTER ENOUGH TIME PASSED, she sneaked up to the bedroom and showered to get ready for dinner. Around six thirty, Dylan walked in. She sat on the bed in a red floor-length, cotton sundress, sliding gold earrings into her earlobes.

"Hey."

She smiled at him. "Hey…" She paused to take a breath. "It looks like we have some things to discuss."

He winced. "You weren't sleeping while Uncle Dom and I were talking, were you?"

"I tried to go back to sleep to give you and your uncle time alone, but the conversation got too interesting."

"Surprised that an almost seventy-year-old confirmed bachelor would want to find someone or that he came right out and asked me if I'd married you to get my stock back?"

"The stock thing. He walked you into a trap."

"I told you he was smart, and I wasn't ruffled by the question. I was more surprised when I thought he'd accepted everything so easily. Now that I know he hasn't, I have a better idea how to handle it."

"What you're saying is that we really have to step up our game."

"Maybe yes. Maybe no. Going overboard will only make him more suspicious."

She rubbed her temples.

"What? Is it that hard to pretend to like me?"

"No."

"Then we just keep going the way we have been, and we'll be fine."

"You're sure?"

"Yes."

"Maybe we should flesh out our story a little more. If your uncle is suspicious, we need more details."

"Like?"

"Like…why me?"

His face scrunched. "Why you?"

Knowing this would be the key to holding their story together, she said, "Why would you choose to marry *me*—not as a ruse but in real life, why would you marry me?"

Thinking, he walked over to the bed where she sat and eased down beside her. "The truth?"

Having him sit so close sent a shower of tingles down her spine, skyrocketing her attraction. She fought to ignore it. "The truth is always what works best."

He pondered for only a second before he said,

"If I were to marry you for real, it would be because you're different."

Her face fell. "Different? That's your criteria for a wife?"

"Not different in a weird way. Different in a comfortable, easygoing way. You're not boring. Just being around each other the short time that we have been I've figured out that you're the kind of woman who'd be happy to go out on a boat or remove your shoes before a beach walk so you could walk in the waves, that kind of thing."

She sniffed. "You didn't figure that out. I took off my shoes Saturday night before we walked on the beach."

He smiled sheepishly. "I also heard the stories about you having a few beers and stepping into a fountain one hot afternoon, and the one about you taking off your shoes on your walk home from the pub one night."

He hadn't just heard them; he remembered them. He remembered *her.* Specifics about her.

Her breath stuttered at the thought that she might have made an impression on him all those years ago. But that was more of a problem than a happy thought. Even considering he might have a real interest in her made her attraction tumble into overdrive. And as much fun as it sounded, she couldn't give in to that. This was a job. A job she needed.

She slid a bit away from him, easing the gesture with a laugh. “Get a little tipsy one time, and step into a fountain and everybody remembers.”

“Don’t forget walking home carrying your shoes.”

She took a breath, forcing herself back to their purpose. “You’re a little too impressed by an old memory. Still, your reasoning for why you would choose me to marry is actually pretty good. I am a go-with-the-flow person. I can’t wait to ride on the boat. I’ll even drink beer and watch you fish. If you tell your uncle that you like me because I’m carefree, he’ll see proof and believe it.” She paused only a second before she asked, “Why else would you marry me?”

“You’re really beautiful.”

Her chest tightened. This was such a bad avenue to pursue but it was unfortunately necessary. “Thank you.”

“And you’re funny. You have this cute dry wit that sneaks out when you’re talking.”

“I try.”

He laughed. “See? There it is. Not silly, just easygoing. I always got the impression that you loved life and people, and that makes you easy to be around.”

“You saw a lot in a few weeks’ worth of Friday nights at a pub while we were at university.”

He shrugged. “Let’s just say being around you again reminded me of things.” He paused a second. "Your turn. Why would you have been interested in me?"

She had been. She'd had an almost crush that had disappeared into nothing when he'd started dating Janine and stopped coming to the pub. She wouldn't mention the crush, but the rest of the truth was good for their story. "Well, you're handsome. And rich."

He clutched his chest. "You married me for my money?"

She sniffed. "No. The ability to make money means you're smart and practical. You took your talents and figured out how to make money with them."

"I did…" He paused, then quietly asked, "Does it bother you that you're having so much trouble finding your way in your career?"

She perked up. "No. Because over the last few days I've been realizing that there's nothing wrong with my business. It was my living arrangements that were off."

"You're going to have to explain that."

"I don't always have a steady income, but I make a decent amount. Unfortunately, I've also been living in a condo that has HOA fees higher than apartment rent in some of the boroughs. Worse, I never had to manage my way through lean years to learn those lessons. I went from my parents' penthouse to a nice condo—that they bought for me. I didn't have the kick in the butt to make myself successful."

He frowned. "You didn't have a mortgage…just HOA fees and you're still struggling?"

"Unfortunately."

"You know, if you sell the condo, you'll have another cushion while you get your business going."

"Can't. While it would be great to add that money to what you're paying me, the condo was a gift from my parents, and I don't feel right selling it and keeping the money. I have to give it back… But that's cool because if I find a cheaper place, I'll have enough money from this job to start over, to give myself time to build up clients and maybe take a marketing class to figure out how to spread the word about my business, not just rely on referrals or my website." She caught his gaze. "You might not believe this, but I'm looking forward to being frugal."

"Looking forward to living in a dive?"

"Not a dive, just somewhere I can afford. That way I can pour every extra cent into making this company work."

He rubbed his hand along his neck. "That actually makes sense."

"Thank you."

His head tilted as he studied her. "You sound surprised that I agree."

She grimaced. "I guess I was just hoping my high society parents take it as well as you did."

He laughed. "See? That's another thing we have in common. We lived that life and don't want it anymore. Luckily, Uncle Dom wasn't as into it as my parents have been. I can put on a tux and drink champagne with the best of them, but it's not who I am. Not who I want to be."

"I always thought of you more like a pirate."

He seemed horrified. "A pirate? Like a thief?"

"No, a suave, confident, sexy university senior ready to take on the world, who wasn't afraid to go after what he wanted."

He smiled. "Now, who's reading things into the few times we were at the same pub with our friends?"

"Well, you could seem to have any woman you wanted."

He chuckled. "Even you?"

"No. I had the start of a crush, but it went away after you left the group."

He shifted closer. "The start of a crush is still a crush. You can't split hairs."

"Don't get excited. That was years ago. And it went away, remember?"

"It's still a nice ego boost."

She inched away from him. "You don't need an ego boost."

"Everybody needs ego boosts. Like I believe in you. You're not exactly making money, but you're not giving up. You're not just pretty and kind, you're smart too. And if you don't think that's sexy, you're wrong." He inched closer. His voice dipped. "You went after what you wanted, too. And from where I'm sitting, you weren't exactly casual about it."

If his nearness and voice weren't enough to seduce her, his words were. He believed in her. Regardless, the conversation about their fake marriage had somehow taken a turn that was a little too real.

She bounced off the bed and walked toward the elevator. "Your uncle is waiting for us."

He snorted but leaned back on the comforter, studying her through narrowed eyes. "I also see you as someone I could come home to and relax with, someone who is probably dynamite in bed."

At the elevator and afraid to turn around and look at him, she laughed nervously. "All good reasons to marry me," she said, bringing the conversation back to its original purpose. But something about both of their imaginings made her chest tight. She reminded herself that he had been play-acting when he came up with reasons why he'd married her. But she'd actually had an almost crush. She was also astute enough to realize he'd turned their simple conversation into flirting.

She remembered him being a flirt before he permanently paired with Janine. Then after her death, she hadn't seen him anywhere. It was as if he'd hidden. Either he'd reverted to his past behavior, or he was enjoying the game. Enjoying teasing her.

Her heart fluttered. Heat washed through her.

She ignored it. With her new decisions about her business, she needed this fee more than ever. She couldn't risk a real romance and mess up this job. She had to keep her head in the game. If she wanted to play her part right and well, she needed to know one more thing.

He rose from the bed and walked toward the bathroom.

"One question before I go."

He faced her.

"How did you and your uncle get so close?"

He frowned.

"Seriously, I need to know. He's going to expect me to know. I don't want him to throw a question at me that I can't answer."

He looked at the ceiling as if thinking that through and finally said, "My uncle and I are close because I lived with him from the time I was fifteen until my business took off and I could afford my own place."

"You didn't live with your parents?"

"My father died, and my mother wasted no time getting remarried—to an oilman from Dallas. When she moved to Texas, I stayed with Uncle Dom because I was still in high school here."

She blinked. "Your dad died?"

"When I was in high school. And it was a relief to live with my uncle. My mother was out of sorts being a widow. Finding a new man gave her purpose again."

She took a breath. She knew all about society wives. She didn't need to make him explain that to her.

"Living with Uncle Dom was easy because we were more like friends."

"I see that."

"Even when I moved out, we still had dinner once a week and spent holidays together."

She could picture it. And living with his uncle wasn't horrible. In a way, it was heartwarming because his uncle had been alone too. "That's nice."

"He is my family."

"What about your mom?"

He shrugged. "She fits in Dallas. Has stepkids. I love her. I went to her big wedding in Dallas; she came to my wedding in Manhattan. But we're not joined at the hip."

She had friends whose parents had divorced who had nontraditional families and nontraditional relationships with their parents. None of that surprised her.

"And it looks like our pretend marriage is a good thing for my uncle. He seems to want to move on too. He might have been a happy bachelor, but I know he gave up things to raise me. Now that he's decided to find someone, I want him to have that."

She thought it through. His uncle had taken him in as a teenager, bought stock in his company before it was worth anything so that Dylan would have start-up cash. He was available for visits and holidays…he *was* Dylan's family. More like a dad than an uncle. It was no wonder he worried Dylan hadn't gotten past the loss of his first marriage. A second marriage, a willingness to try again, might have been what he'd wanted to see from Dylan.

She felt a bit of guilt for the marriage that wasn't going to last but also considered that what Uncle Dom really needed was a little reassurance that Dylan was okay. A short-term marriage wasn't the best way to do that, but a week together was. And maybe her real job was to simply show his uncle that Dylan was happy.

After all, that was what he really wanted. For his nephew to be happy.

"Okay." She turned toward the elevator again. "I'll go downstairs, and if he's already there, I'll entertain him."

He stopped her by catching her hand. "No. Wait for me. I think we should make an entrance together."

The intimate contact made her melt a little bit inside. They might have been discussing things she needed to know for the ruse, but those discussions meant she was getting to know him, and he was beginning to trust her. He was a charming, handsome, likable guy who cared enough to ask about her career, her future.

He released her hand and headed for the bathroom and his closet. She shook her head. While she could easily spend the week showing Dylan's uncle that he was happy just the way he was, whether Dylan was likable or not was irrelevant. This time next week, she would be apartment hunting and planning how she would give back the condo her parents had bought her. That gift was part of their plan for her life—which she had rejected. She needed to let it go to move on.

Her time with Dylan wasn't supposed to be personal. She was doing a job. Not forming lasting bonds. This week was a stepping stone to getting her life together, as much as giving back her condo, finding an apartment and living in a way she could afford.

Satisfied that she was on the right track, she rose when Dylan reentered the bedroom wearing a short-sleeved shirt and dressy shorts. "Ready?"

"Yes."

They entered the elevator and made their way to the first floor. "We'll check the patio. He probably grabbed a beer and is watching the ocean."

As they opened the sliding glass door to the pool area where, as predicted, Uncle Dom stood by the stone wall looking out over the sea, Dylan said, "Hey, you beat us."

He displayed his beer. "Hope you don't mind."

"My house is your house." He turned to Lilibet. "What can I get you?"

"A beer is fine."

Uncle Dom laughed. "I like that. Nothing snooty."

"I have my nights when I like snooty drinks. Tonight, at the beach…" She breathed in the salty air. "Beer suits."

The old man walked over and relaxed on a patio chair. "So, tell me a little bit about yourself."

Not surprised by the question, she said, "Well, I work in New York." She considered telling him about her parents but didn't want to give him any avenues to investigate her. "There's really not much more to me than that. I'm a simple girl. I work. I lived alone—" she glanced over at Dylan, giving him an intimate look "—until I met Dylan."

"Trust me," Dom said. "Simple is better. I'm looking for someone like that."

Dylan walked over to her chair and handed her a beer. "I know you'll think I'm crazy, but that's why I like it here. Life is simple."

"Life is simple with your houseful of servants?" Uncle Dom scoffed.

"You forget. I work. Sometimes twelve hours a day. I don't want to cook or clean. I like quiet nights listening to the ocean, sleeping in on Sundays, doing crosswords."

She smiled at the picture that formed in her mind. He'd spent his youth being part of New York

City society, and he was done with it. In a way, that had sort of happened to her. Charity balls with her parents from the time she was sixteen. Gallery showings of up-and-coming artists, rubbing elbows with the city's elite. Hearing people talk about business deals and their summer homes. They supported enough charities to prove they cared, but they liked fine china, crystal glasses, limousines and exclusive restaurants.

She liked bagels.

Even if she had liked that life, she hadn't felt she fit in.

As his uncle chatted away with Lilibet, Dylan tried to stop thinking about their conversation on the bed. Not because it had been a while since he'd flirted. But because it had felt different. So natural he couldn't stop himself.

Still, they were both playing a role, but, for a while, he hadn't been. His common sense had turned off and his fun side had kicked in, and he'd let himself run with it, if only because totally relaxing with a woman was a breath of fresh air, something he hadn't done in forever.

Nonetheless, this was a job to her, evidenced by the fact that she'd kept shifting away from him, not playing along, when they were alone. Still, something about the way she'd called him a sexy pirate had given him a jolt of attraction he couldn't seem to wish away. Women had always seen him as sexy. But how she'd said it had felt real. Most of what was between them was made up, yet that exchange somehow felt genuine.

His uncle continued in his talkative mood, one minute appearing to subtly interrogate Lilibet, and the next excitedly talking about a woman in his building who'd been a widow for a few years.

Dylan kept watching Lilibet. How she ate dinner with gusto. How she truly enjoyed Uncle Dom's company. She smiled. She laughed. She drank wine, refilling glasses when anyone's glass was empty like she belonged in his dining room, happily talking with his uncle.

Around midnight, Dom excused himself to go to bed and Dylan led Lilibet to the elevator. Too confused to talk, he rode up to his room in silence and he let her use the bathroom first. When she came out in another pair of fully covering pajamas, he went in. He didn't make the mistake of wearing sweats. He put on a T-shirt and shorts. He let the sliding doors open, didn't adjust the thermostat, so they wouldn't get too cold and gravitate together.

He lifted the covers. Lilibet lay on her side, facing the open doors. He slid under the sheet and comforter. In case she was still awake, he said, "Good night."

She quietly replied, "Good night."

Though he didn't want to make awkward conversation, he did feel he should tell her she'd done well at dinner. That might even bring them back to normal footing. In fact, if he looked at the time they were forced to spend together in his bedroom as debriefing time, he might minimize his attraction and remind himself of what they were really doing together.

"It was a nice night. You were perfect. Casual, as if we'd been together for years."

"It was easy. Your uncle's great." She shifted so she was lying on her back.

"He is…" He looked sideways at her. "And he likes you." He sat up. "That's a big deal. He's a great guy, but it usually takes him a while to warm up to people."

She sat up too. "So, do you think he's warmed up to the woman in his building?"

"Definitely. He said she's been a widow for years. He's probably been mulling this over that whole time."

She laughed. "That's adorable."

"He was a confirmed bachelor. Either he really is lonely or she's special." He shook his head. "Either way, this is going to be fun to watch."

"How are you going to watch that relationship from a beach house thousands of miles away?"

He smiled devilishly. "First, I'll video call when I think they might be on a date. When he gets wise to that, I'll make surprise visits so I can horn in on their time together. Tease them a bit."

"That's mean!"

"What do you think this visit of his was about? He's checking up. Trying to catch me in a lie. Plus, he did worse to me when I was first dating in high school." He drew a satisfied breath. "It feels like playful payback."

She laughed. "After any third date, my parents would insist the man in my life have dinner with the family. They'd grill him then I swear they graded him and gave me assessment lectures."

Dylan chortled. "Now, that's funny."

"It took me years to catch on to the fact that I should keep my dates to myself. Now, when they ask if I'm dating, I say, nope. Still single."

A weird sensation crept through him. It had never occurred to him that she might be dating someone. He should feel remorse that he'd dragged her into his plan without asking if she had someone in her life. Instead, he was glad she was here, with him, not in New York with some other guy. He reminded himself that this was just a job to her, but couldn't help asking, "So, you keep your love life a secret?"

"A wise daughter of overbearing parents always does. Though right now there's nothing to hide. The past year I've been so focused on my business that if anybody was interested in me, I was too preoccupied to see it."

Relief automatically flitted through him, and he had to stifle a sigh. Tomorrow he would work harder at making this room a safe place, a place where they conducted the business of making their charade a success.

Right now, it was best to stop talking, stop thinking before they stepped over any lines. He moved away, sliding down to put his head on his pillow. “Good night.”

She whispered, “Good night.”

The room fell silent. The sound of the ocean waves lapping at the shore drifted to him. He closed his eyes and smiled in the darkness. Business deal or not, he couldn’t remember the last time he’d had a fun night like the one they’d had tonight. Good conversation. His uncle bubbly and happy. And a very nice woman somehow making it special.

Because it was her job. He might miss her when she left, but she *would* leave. Her life was in New York. Even if he wanted to change that, he wouldn’t. He’d sworn off relationships. Partly for himself and partly for the women he dated. He would never again hurt anyone the way he’d hurt Janine.

He had an entire week and two holidays to enjoy her company. And he could—if he kept his wits about him and remembered their relationship had a shelf life. When their marriage ended, he wouldn’t seek her out. When it was over, it would be over.

But accepting that gave him the leeway to enjoy her while he had her here.

Because she'd liked him all those years ago. She'd called it an almost crush, but that didn't change it.

She'd liked him.

CHAPTER EIGHT

LILIBET SAT IN one of the club chairs by the open doors, laptop on her thighs, when Dylan woke the next morning. He sat up like a bolt of lightning and scowled at her.

"What are you doing?"

"Checking my email."

He ran his hand down his face. "Sun isn't up yet…so it's not even six o'clock! Besides, computers aren't allowed in my bedroom."

She found that hard to believe. "Really? You never work up here?"

"Never."

She snorted. Uncurling herself from the chair, she said, "What about your phone…that has a computer."

He lifted his phone from the bedside table. "This is my private phone. Only twelve people have the number. Most of them family. If someone calls me on this phone in the middle of the night, it's an emergency, and I want to answer. Business phone is in the office at night."

"But what if there's a crisis in the Asian markets while you're sleeping?"

He shrugged. "Someone will handle it."

"But what if they can't?"

"Have you ever heard of the concept of something being meant to be?"

Looking at him leaning against the headboard in his pristine white T-shirt, with his dark hair disheveled and his handsome face relaxed, something tweaked inside her. When she'd met him at university, she'd had a sense of destiny, but he'd gone off with Janine, and she hadn't even let her feelings turn into a full-blown crush. Just an almost crush.

But right in this minute, with him talking about things that were meant to be, the sense returned on a wave of longing. It short-circuited her breathing and filled her head with thoughts of how special her life could be with him. Someone who understood her. Someone easygoing yet focused. Someone so sexy just looking at him made her breath stutter.

Reminding herself of the futility of thinking that way, she blocked those images.

"When I discovered my talent for helping people, I'd thought my being a problem solver was meant to be, but you see how that's working out."

"You know, most successful businesspeople are problem solvers."

She laughed. "What?"

"Think about it. I have accountants to keep track of the numbers. I just review them, looking for trouble and coming up with answers to fix them. Same with engineers, operations managers and plant managers. They submit reports detailing the good and the bad. I study the bad and offer solutions based on what's right for the company, the deal or the product, then they implement those solutions." He shrugged. "Technically, I'm a fixer too."

"My problem-solving is more personal. That's the part of the work that draws me."

"If you like getting personal with people, you would be a great human resources director."

She sniffed.

"Too good to work in an office?"

"No. I just—" The thought of having a real job with a reliable salary settled in her brain comfortably, confusing her. It would be nice to get a regular paycheck and never have to wonder where her next money was coming from. Still, she said, "I just always saw myself outside of an office environment, doing things."

"Too much of a free spirit?"

"I don't know."

"I think you spent so much time not wanting to work for your parents that you couldn't consider any possibility other than being your own boss." He studied her for a second. "Why didn't you want to work for your parents?"

She answered without thinking. "Aside from hating the idea of spending twelve hours a day writing briefs and researching law, I believed that if they were my bosses, I'd always be a kid, the baby of the family. Never a grown-up."

"Ah. There it is. You really don't want to work for yourself. You wanted something different than working for your parents. You could probably find that in an existing company, especially as a human resources director. You might have to take some classes and maybe even start at the bottom and work your way up the corporate ladder but think of all the people you would meet. All the fun you could have listening to their problems, helping them get ahead in their careers."

Though she hated to admit it, that did sound fun. "That's interesting."

"Something to think about. And I'm here if you need to talk about it more." He rolled out of bed. "Don't shower this morning. My uncle wants to go fishing. If you come with us, you'll be baking in the sun, sweating, and need another shower when we return."

She laughed. It had felt good to get advice about her life from someone who didn't have a stake in the outcome. She would never have believed the easygoing guy she'd met at university could be so serious, then she remembered he'd started and now ran four software companies. That would make a guy pretty serious. On top of that, he'd lost his wife. He had to have changed after losing the most important person in his world. Especially since he seemed to have recovered—

Or had he? Moving away from Manhattan—the city in which he'd been married—might not have been because he loved the beach but because he'd needed to get away from reminders. No computers or phones in the bedroom might mean nothing more than a division of his business and personal lives, not great emotional growth. He'd said he didn't ever want to marry again. A person who'd truly recovered wouldn't be inflexible. Maybe all this wasn't so much recovery as it was hiding?

It didn't matter. He'd given her good advice. They'd had a nice chat. She shouldn't ruin it by overthinking something that was none of her business. After all, this wasn't a real relationship.

When Dylan walked out of the bathroom dressed in swim trunks and a T-shirt, she closed her laptop.

"Don't forget. Wear a bathing suit and something to cover up to protect you from the sun in case you fall asleep." At the bedroom door he added, "Or maybe bring a book unless you want Uncle Dom to teach you to fish."

Happiness unexpectedly filled her. She liked his uncle and couldn't remember the last time she was out on a boat. Weird as it sounded, having a good time this morning was part of her job.

"Actually, learning to fish might be fun."

"Good. He'll love that."

After he left, she put on a swimsuit and cover-up and raced downstairs. Before she went to the dining room, she took her laptop to the office where she and Dylan had spoken to his uncle the day after their wedding. She found an open spot on the desk for her little computer and the oddest sensation wobbled through her. Her laptop fit on his desk, as if there was a place for her.

She shook her head at the silliness of that. First, she had exactly seventeen inches on his desk. Not a place in his life. Second, did she really want a place in his life? Especially now, when things in her own life were finally making sense? And things about his life were beginning to confuse her?

No.

But she did want to go fishing and she did want to relax.

There was nothing wrong with forgetting about the bad for a while to enjoy the good.

She walked into the dining room and one of Chef Alice's people was immediately at her side, pouring her a cup of coffee. She asked for a lightly toasted bagel and the young woman left.

Uncle Dom said, "Okay, I'm just going to come right out with this. It took me until this morning to realize I barged in on your honeymoon."

Dylan laughed. "You didn't barge in on our honeymoon. We invited you."

"It's still your honeymoon."

"Actually, we're thinking about going to Paris in the spring."

Dylan's gaze jumped to hers. His eyebrows rose sky high. She smiled in a way she hoped reminded him they would be divorced by then. He didn't have to go to Paris.

Uncle Dom said, "Isn't that around the time of your annual board of directors meeting?"

Without missing a beat, Dylan said, "We'll go when it's over, of course. I'll probably need the break after everything that goes into that."

Uncle Dom sighed. "I didn't screw up your plans?"

"No!" Dylan said emphatically. "And that's the end of serious talk. We're going fishing. Lilibet wants you to teach her to fish."

Uncle Dom brightened. "You don't say?"

Lilibet said, "Hey, if I'm going to live here, I want to enjoy it. Fishing, boating, water skiing… everything."

"Well, all right!" Uncle Dom tossed his napkin to the table and rose. "I'll change into my swimming trunks. I'll be back in ten minutes, and we can get going."

The morning turned out to be perfect. Fishing itself wasn't too difficult, and Lilibet could see why people liked it. The ocean was calm, a beautiful teal color that reflected the sun and necessitated three times the sunblock than what she typically used. They returned tired and hungry. Uncle Dom opted for a nap before food, and Dylan caught her hand to stop her before she went inside.

"I'm taking a swim to cool off before we change for lunch. Want to join me?"

Temptation was nearly overwhelming. She'd never been as happy as she was with him. But that was the reason she needed to keep some distance. Reality too often sneaked into their situation. His helping her with her business like someone who was genuinely interested. Her wondering about him, his life, as if they were friends. Getting to know each other for the ruse was causing them to actually get to know each other.

They needed some distance.

She shook her head. "I was thinking of going inside to check my emails before I change."

"Eager to see if you have new business?"

"Yes," she replied honestly. "It's all part of my is-this-business-really-going-anywhere evaluation. By the way, I put my laptop in your office, so I don't violate your no-computers-in-the-bedroom policy."

He laughed. "Thank you."

"Hey, anything to please the hubby who is taking me to Paris."

He laughed again.

Before she had time to think it through, she rose and kissed his cheek. "See you in the dining room in about twenty minutes."

* * *

She walked into the house and Dylan watched her go. He knew she hadn't been faking the fun she'd had that morning on the boat. That pleased him more than it should have. But he'd also noticed that his uncle wasn't the frail old man Dylan had worried he was becoming. And he was falling for someone, looking for companionship. He was mentally and physically stable.

Dylan had never been so happy. He'd plotted his marriage to Lilibet to get his stock back. Instead, it felt as if things in his life were righting themselves. He hadn't thought anything was askew, but he had to admit he'd been concerned about his uncle aging. Now he wasn't.

He would give Lilibet the credit for that except she wouldn't be here if he hadn't made the marriage plan. He'd simply made a very good choice with her.

He took off his shirt and dove into the deep end of the swimming pool enjoying the cool water. He swam for twenty minutes and ambled to his room expecting to see Lilibet there. When she wasn't, he changed into shorts and a T-shirt, confused about where she could be. The last thing she'd told him was that she planned to check her emails, then she'd see him in the dining room.

Hoping she'd gotten lucky and found work, he went to his office to look for her. He entered the room and immediately saw she was on a video call with an older gentleman with gray hair.

"And who is this?" the man demanded as Dylan stopped in the doorway.

Lilibet whipped around. "Oh, that's—"

The man on the computer screen squinted and said, "Wait. Is that Dylan Olsen?"

"Yes, Dad."

Dylan thought three things at once. Her dad was checking up on her. Meaning, Lilibet hadn't been the one to place the call. Her dad had called her. And Dylan had no idea how they were supposed to play this.

He'd already realized she probably hadn't told her parents she'd married him as a job, so he wouldn't mention it.

"Hello, Mr. McDonald," he said, walking closer to the small laptop screen. "It's nice to meet you."

"It is amazing to meet you! What crazy thing does my daughter have you doing?"

"Nothing," Lilibet answered for him. "Actually, I'm here on something of a vacation. I'm taking a bit of time to think through my next steps with the business."

"And I'm helping her," Dylan stated to justify his presence.

"*You're* helping her? That's great!" He clapped his hands together in glee. "I didn't even know you knew each other."

"We were at university together," Lilibet said. "He graduated a few years before I did."

Her dad could not contain his joy. "This is wonderful!"

"Yeah, well," Lilibet said. "We're about to have a late lunch so maybe we can talk when I'm back in New York."

"Yes! We will!" He looked past her. "It was a pleasure to meet you, Mr. Olsen."

"Dylan, please," Dylan said. "It was a pleasure to meet you too."

He disconnected the call. Lilibet slammed her laptop closed and ran her hands down her face.

"What happened there?"

She peeked at him through her fingers. "I was looking things up on the internet and suddenly he called. He was checking on me. His deadline for my business performing better has passed. I'm sure he called to remind me I'd promised to go to law school if my company hadn't succeeded in five years. But you came in the room just in time to save me."

"And now he thinks we're friends. Just buddies on vacation." He paused. "You didn't tell your parents we'd gotten married, did you?"

She blew out a sigh. "No. I thought it better, easier, if I didn't. It might be a real marriage, but we didn't make anything more than a four-month commitment to each other. I do not want to have to explain to my dad, who clearly knows who you are and adores you, why I divorced you."

A real sense of what she'd done for him stole through him. She wasn't just giving up a week and going on two dates; this marriage impacted her life.

She shook her head. "This has got to be the weirdest week."

And he didn't want her to carry their serious mood out to the patio with his uncle. While he respected her right to keep this marriage a secret, here on the island, with his uncle, they needed to be happy.

"It's turning out to be a good week for me. First, I feel like I'm getting my uncle back. Second, if I help you think through your future, your dad will be placated and never even suspect we're married. Third, you learned how to fish today."

She chuckled. "It's certainly not the week I envisioned."

"Sometimes that's better. Now, go change. I'm going to tell the kitchen to make us sandwiches. Anything you like?"

"Egg salad."

"See you in twenty minutes."

"Okay."

He turned to leave but she stopped him. "Thank you for helping me with my dad."

He thought for a second. "You know, when we started this, I needed your help. And you were always on top of things. Feels good to return the favor."

Their gazes met in the silent room as everything between them changed. It was as if he was really seeing her for the first time. Not as an answer to a problem, but as a person. Someone he liked, whose company he enjoyed, who made the day happier somehow. The truth of that rushed through him. He liked her, *knew her.*

She smiled.

He smiled. He could not remember the last time he'd felt like this. Janine might have bowled him over, but it had been work to woo her. They had not enjoyed the same things so one of them had always compromised.

He shook his head to clear it. What was he doing thinking of Janine, comparing her to Lilibet? A real romance wasn't in the cards for him and Lilibet for a million different reasons. The most important of which being that he didn't want another romance. Memories of his unhappy marriage and Janine's death bombarded him. Not just his pain, but Janine's.

He was responsible for both.

And he did not want to go through that again. Especially not with someone as wonderful as Lilibet. She deserved better.

He walked out of his office without another word.

When he was gone, Lilibet squeezed her eyes shut and reminded herself that this was a job, the feelings weren't real, but the reminder didn't penetrate considering the interest she'd seen in his eyes. Unfortunately, that only resurrected the original reason to stick to her role and not get in over her head. Dylan had no intention of having another serious relationship. There'd be no changing his mind, and she wasn't the kind of person to enter trouble willingly. In a way, that's why she didn't want to go to law school. Working at a job she hated would be terrible. She'd spent five years resisting her parents' suggestions, nagging and downright pushing. Surely she could resist a handsome, kind, genius who didn't want to fall in love again?

She raised her hands and counted off the days left for his uncle's weeklong visit on her fingers. Five days. That's all she had left. She could be strong for five days.

After lunch, she put on a bathing suit and headed to the pool, which was empty. Knowing Uncle Dom was undoubtedly still napping, and Dylan had gone to his office to work, she slid into the cool water and swam across the pool. When she finished swimming, she stretched out on the chaise to take her own nap.

Less than a minute later, she heard someone open the doors to come onto the patio. She opened her eyes just enough to see it was Dylan. He caught the back of a chaise lounge and dragged it over beside hers. Then he sat down, got comfortable and closed his eyes.

She didn't wonder why he'd brought his chaise beside hers. It was part of their charade. Nothing more than that.

She settled more deeply into her chair, mimicking his moves to get comfortable. She drifted into a light sleep and woke an hour later to the sound of the door opening and closing again.

She sat up. "Uncle Dom."

He yawned and stretched. "I get the best naps here."

She laughed. "Me too."

Dylan stirred.

Dom said, "Good. You're up."

Dylan cleared his throat. "Sort of."

"I'm going to take a swim, but before I do—" he handed Dylan a small card "—I made a reservation for you at…" He named a restaurant by the water, relaxed and not overly fancy.

Dylan glanced up at him. "For all of us?"

"No. For you and Lilibet." He batted his hand. "I know. I know. Your real honeymoon is Paris in the spring. But you're newly married and don't need me by your side for everything."

Lilibet looked at him. "You're leaving?"

"Oh, hell no. I'm having too much fun. I'm just giving you and my nephew some space."

She smiled. "Thank you. But you're no trouble. We like having you around."

He bent and kissed her forehead. "And I want to be invited back so I'm on best behavior."

She laughed and Uncle Dom's face glowed. She noticed Dylan giving him a strange look. It wasn't an expression she'd ever seen from him before, and she couldn't interpret it.

But that was the second piece of odd behavior from him that afternoon. First, he'd really looked at her—and saw her, not as the problem solver he'd hired but just plain Lilibet McDonald—then he'd walked away. Now, he'd reacted in a way she couldn't interpret.

Something was going on with him. Part of her knew she should confront him, make sure it wasn't something that might ruin his ruse. The other part worried that he was beginning to wonder about the same things she was, the biggest being their attraction.

After all, they had to sleep in the same bed for five more nights.

CHAPTER NINE

For the rest of the afternoon, Lilibet didn't mention the strange way Dylan had been looking at her and his uncle. But seated outside on the huge deck of a seaside restaurant, the scent of grilling food competing with the salty air that drifted on the light breeze, she knew she wouldn't find a better time to discuss it. Especially if she had to remind him to control some of his reactions.

"I don't want to be mean but I'm glad your uncle isn't with us so we can discuss a few things."

Dressed simply in a short-sleeved shirt and dress pants with his hair blowing in the breeze, Dylan didn't look like a billionaire businessman. He looked like a guy who liked the ocean and had embraced the salt life—the world he'd created for himself.

"Are you kidding? He was so happy to have done something nice for you that he about burst the seams of his shirt."

"You mean, he was so proud of doing something nice for *us*."

Dylan shook his head. "In two short days, I think he's beginning to like you more than me."

She laughed. She'd sensed his uncle liked her, but the depth of his feelings must have surprised Dylan, which explained the weird look, and meant she didn't have to ask him about it. "I like him too." But her conscience tweaked. In some ways, the more successful they were with this temporary marriage, the more possibility they'd hurt Uncle Dom when they divorced.

The waiter arrived with the wine they'd ordered and poured some for each of them.

As he left, Dylan offered his glass for a toast. "To our successful marriage."

She shook her head as she touched her glass to his. "I'm worried that the more successful we are at convincing Uncle Dom, the more disappointed he'll be when we break up."

"He'll be knee-deep in his relationship with the widow by then. Happiness about her will diminish his disappointment in us."

She sighed. "So, you've said."

"The real wild card here is your dad. He doesn't look like the kind of guy to sit idly by. We led him to believe we were good friends…or dating. Is there any reason we should worry he'll come to Belize and check up on you? You'd said he and your mom used to invite boyfriends to dinner—could he drop in on us?"

She thought for a minute. "More than likely

he'll casually call again, probe to ascertain the details about our relationship and then invite you to dinner."

"Either way, I get a dinner out of this."

She sniffed a laugh. "He'll invite you to their penthouse. Meaning, you'd have to be in Manhattan to accept, and you live here. There's nothing to worry about. All we have to do is tell him that you don't know when you'll be in the city next, because you work from home and live *here*." She glanced around at the beauty of the sea and the palm trees, and reverently said, "You live *here*."

He laughed. "I am lucky."

She tilted her head. Even though the question that popped into her head was legitimate, she hesitated. He wouldn't want to discuss his personal life, and the question didn't really relate to their ruse.

Still, curiosity got the better of her and she said, "You know, another problem solver might wonder if you aren't really hiding here."

"From what?"

He sounded neither angry nor insulted, so she said, "Bad memories. Reminders of your old life. Curious parents of women you're dating."

He chuckled. "That could be part of it. But you were out on that boat this morning. You saw how nice it is to start the day that way. Then swim. Then sleep in the sun." He motioned around the deck area. "Then come someplace like this and eat a fabulous meal."

"Outside."

"What?"

"The first day we were here, we ate in your dining room because you don't like to eat outside."

"No, I said food should be eaten in a dining room." He motioned around again. "This is a dining room."

"I think you're splitting hairs."

"Okay. How about this? Because I always eat inside, coming to places like this is special."

"You really do think everything through, don't you?"

"Yes."

"And you're happier because of it?"

"That's the only reason to think everything through."

She studied his dark eyes for a second and knew there was another reason to think everything through. He'd had some surprises in his life that hurt him, things he couldn't control. The loss of his wife. The loss of his father. His mother remarrying, then leaving him with his uncle. Now that Lilibet knew more about his past, she didn't think his need for control was wrong or even odd. It was a defense mechanism. It also didn't hurt anyone. Only kept his life moving smoothly.

"That makes sense."

"You thought I was going to deny that insulating myself was part of the reason I moved here."

Actually, she shouldn't have been surprised he'd admitted the truth. Whether he knew it or not, he'd begun to trust her. Not just with her ability to navigate their marriage but with information about himself. His real self. And not merely because he needed her. Forced proximity was making him comfortable. Maybe too comfortable.

After they ordered dinner, she kept the conversation on her family. She didn't push him to give additional details about himself because the more comfortable he got with her, the more comfortable she got with him, and they still had to sleep in the same bed that night. A little dose of information every day for the next few days would be plenty to keep the charade tight, and not so much they got in too deep.

The drive home with the top down on his convertible was wonderful. She put her head back and breathed in the fresh air. Laughing, they got out of the car in the driveway and strolled toward the house. Hearing music from the back patio they walked through the long hall to the French doors and found Uncle Dom lying on a chaise, beer in hand, staring at the ocean, listening to the soft strains of songs from an era long before her time.

"Big bands?" Dylan asked. "Aren't you a little young for that?"

Dom laughed. "I was a crossover kid. Listened

to big bands while my parents controlled the radio, and the Beatles when I got a transistor radio for my room." He took a breath. "Tell me the big band sound doesn't suit the mood. Soft. Mellow. Peaceful."

Dylan looked around. "I guess it does."

Dom sat up. "How was dinner?"

"Oh, lovely!" Lilibet said. "Thank you."

He rose from his chaise. "Letting you go alone is what family does…they're considerate."

Given her parents' insistence that she go to law school, she might debate that. But Uncle Dom rose and headed to the door. "I'm turning in." He glanced back. "You two should dance."

After he was inside and walking up the hall to the elevator, Dylan laughed. "If we weren't already married, I would worry that he was fixing us up. But maybe he's still testing us."

She smiled at the door. "No. He's just a nice guy."

He caught her hand and eased her into a dance hold. "Oh, yeah? And you know this how?"

She fell into step with the soft slow song that came from the phone Uncle Dom had apparently left on the small table by his chaise lounge. She wouldn't argue with a little dancing. Dylan could be right. His uncle could still be testing them, hoping to trip them up when he returned for his phone. Dancing made them look like a happily married couple.

Smooth notes from a clarinet mixed and mingled with the soft sea breeze. The skirt of her long sundress shifted with every move they made.

Dylan sighed. "This really is nice. Relaxing."

"That's why he suggested it. Maybe not to trip you up, but to give you a break." She frowned. "Though you haven't seemed to have worked too hard these past couple of days."

He sighed, as if tired. "This week my work isn't about quantity but weight. I made a decision about one of my companies this morning that will haunt me if it's wrong."

He usually talked about his companies so casually that she never thought about the pressure of his work. Anybody who dealt in billions of dollars had stress, if only because their decisions affected everyone from his uncle to his employees.

She winced. "Well, that's not good."

He twirled her around. "No. That's business. It's the risks that make us." He pulled her into his arms again and dipped her. "And the ability to rebound that determines if we're a success or a failure." He brought her back up.

"I've heard my dad say something similar a time or two."

"You do realize that your parents' law firm is a business. They deal with profit and loss, marketing, human resources, everything required to manage the firm, on top of taking cases, meeting clients, researching law, creating strategy, writing briefs, going to court…"

She took a breath, trying to focus on what he was saying but it just felt so right being held by him, swaying to music, twirling in the dim light of a patio by the ocean.

She forced her brain back to the conversation. "Are you telling me that I don't have to be a lawyer to find a place in their firm? Or that I shouldn't be so hard on them for trying to drag me over to the dark side?"

"Both… But I might also add that I wonder if they don't just simply like having you around. Maybe your dad didn't call to check up on you but because he misses you. Maybe they want to spend more time with you…and work is the easy way to do that because that's where they are most of the time?"

Their dancing slowed to a stop, but he still held her, still gazed into her eyes. "It's not so hard to believe that they like you and miss you. *I* like you. Probably ten times more than I did when we met all those years ago. Being around you is equal parts of relaxing and fun."

She couldn't release his gaze, couldn't pull out of his hold. Their attraction suddenly felt stronger, more magnetic than it ever had.

To save herself, she whispered, "You and I argue a lot. It wasn't easy to get you to behave the way you needed to."

He snorted. "That wasn't arguing. I prefer to think of it as sorting through things. I had no idea what this marriage would entail. I saw it as a means to an end. You saw the details, the things I missed. Technically, I love that you make my life easier."

"That's my job, remember?" Her voice was soft and tentative. He liked her. The feminine side of her shivered with longing. The practical side shivered with apprehension. This was a job for her, a mission for him. It was fine for them to like each other. But she liked him a lot. And now he was admitting he liked her too—

Of course, he might not mean romantically. He was discussing her parents' business when he'd said it.

He smiled. "True, it's your job. But I haven't discovered anything about you that I don't like. You're not even a cover hog."

Their gazes stayed connected. She watched as confusion suddenly filled his eyes. As if he only now realized the depth of what he was saying. He had to know that taking this conversation even one step further could be trouble, could ruin their plan to get his stock back. But, if he was reminding himself of that, he would release her. Then tease her. Maybe offer her a drink or a walk on the beach.

Instead, he kept looking at her, his eyes so serious that she had to wonder if he wasn't considering the consequences of breaking his rule not to get involved again or his failures in his difficult marriage.

All his fault.

He stepped away, releasing her, then glanced around casually as if the moment hadn't happened. "Should we have a beer? Maybe take a walk on the beach?"

She could have laughed at the way she could read him, but disappointment swamped her. She told herself that was foolish, and tried to pull herself together, but the feelings lingered. Even as the businessperson in her didn't want to do anything to risk the success of this project, the part of her that she'd been ignoring for years couldn't shake the regret. Her future rose or fell based on the completion of this job, but she was so tired of her entire life revolving around finding work, pleasing clients and struggling with her HOA fees that she suddenly wanted to shed it all and just be herself for one night.

One wonderful romantic night with a handsome, sexy, smart, kind man.

But with her business floundering, she couldn't risk that. If she pushed this—pushed him—in the morning, there would be consequences.

She'd always known it. She simply hadn't realized she was so vulnerable.

She backed off. "Let's have a beer." A moonlit walk on the beach seemed too romantic and having a beer together made them seem more like buddies than two people fighting an attraction.

"Sounds good."

He headed toward the bar, but the music stopped when the phone began to ring. Dylan turned to face it, walked over to the little table by the chaise and glanced down at caller ID. "It's Uncle Dom."

"Calling his phone from his other phone?" she asked, totally confused, but his uncle having two phones was the only explanation if his name popped up on caller ID. Of course, Dylan had two phones. One for business. One personal.

"That's what it looks like."

Dylan picked up the ringing phone. "I better take this up to him." He sent the call to voicemail and tucked the phone in his pocket before walking to the door. "Actually, I'm sort of tired so I'm just going to bed. You can stay down here as long as you like."

When he was gone, Lilibet gathered her purse and went inside too. Hoping Dylan would spend a minute or two with his uncle, she slipped into the foyer and upstairs.

She changed into pajamas and tucked herself into bed, shaking her head. This truly was turning out to be the oddest week of her life. So much of it was good and easy. She liked Dylan. He was a smart, congenial guy. She liked his effervescent uncle. Dylan was also helping her to sort through her business troubles. Her dad was happy. *She* had never been happier.

She simply couldn't have the man who was making it all happen. Not when she knew—deep down—that he wasn't the kind of guy to change his mind about his big life decisions. He'd decided he would never enter another serious relationship and the emotions swirling through her when they were together were feeling more and more serious by the minute.

Maybe that's what troubled her the most. Not jeopardizing her job but losing her heart only to get it broken.

By the time he came to the room, she was already in bed and able to pretend she was sleeping. There would be no more risk of romance or consequences.

After tonight, she only had four days until she went home.

CHAPTER TEN

As he walked by the bed, Dylan took enough of a glance to recognize Lilibet was either pretending to sleep or actually sleeping. Which was fine. He couldn't explain what happened when they were dancing except that his defenses had completely fallen.

He couldn't believe it, yet he could. She was sweet, happy, easy to get to know and to like. He'd meant what he'd said about her parents missing her and looking for ways to be around her because he'd never met anyone like her. She liked his uncle, she liked his home, she liked *him.* Just as he was.

Everything had been a struggle with Janine. Debates that led to compromises, compromises that forced him to make subtle changes that led to him refusing to do certain things—especially with her family—until she'd stopped asking for his attention, and he hadn't seen that she wasn't compromising. They were at the beginning of the end of their marriage.

It would be convenient to believe that the differences between Janine and Lilibet could mean a relationship with her would be totally different, but he was the wild card. He was the one who worked too much. He was the one who'd made their marriage difficult.

He walked into the bathroom to change, shaking his head. He couldn't believe he'd basically gotten reacquainted with this woman a few days ago and he was having thoughts of permanency and marriage, particularly since his abysmal relationship skills were what damaged his first marriage.

He had to remember that.

He had to keep his uncle happy.

He had to get his stock back.

And he had to keep the promise to himself that he'd never hurt anyone else the way he'd hurt Janine.

Because it was the woman that he liked so very much that he'd be hurting.

And that was the real bottom line. He liked Libet too much to hurt her.

In his shorts and T-shirt again, he crawled into bed. She stirred weakly, a sure sign she was asleep. He stifled a laugh. He'd seriously never met anyone who could sleep the way she did. It was equally humorous and endearing, and part of him wanted to cuddle into her or gently kiss her cheek.

But he didn't. His reasons for leaving her alone were sound. He didn't have to ponder anymore. He had to behave himself.

He awoke alone the next morning. Sitting up, he listened for the sounds of the shower or someone puttering around in the bathroom but heard nothing. He rolled out of bed, quickly rinsed off under the multiple sprays in his walk-in shower, dressed casually and headed downstairs.

Lilibet sat in the dining room eating a bagel, reading her phone. She wore an airy floral blouse, jeans and flip-flops. Her hair had been pulled into a ponytail that formed a long, loose yellow curl that reached her back.

Everything inside him flickered to life. She was pretty, smart and fun. He didn't want to have to resist her. But he also didn't want to mislead her or, worse, hurt her.

She glanced up when she heard him. "Good morning."

He walked to his seat. Her greeting wasn't exactly cool, but it wasn't warm and friendly either. He considered that those few minutes he'd been so tempted while dancing with her the night before had made her cautious. So he would go back to playing his role.

"Good morning." He kissed her quickly, hopefully the way a smitten husband greeted his wife. "Where's Uncle Dom?"

"He went upstairs to get ready to go fishing this morning. He said he'll meet you on the back patio."

He motioned to her frilly blouse, not something

a smart person wore to fish in. "Is that how you're going out on the boat?"

Her soft, warm laugh brought a ripple of relief. He might have made her cautious the night before, but she'd accepted the good morning kiss for what it was and easily slipped into her role.

"I'm not going fishing."

He frowned. "I thought you liked the boat."

"I do…but I got an email from a potential client. We're video calling this morning. Hopefully, the request is something I can handle." Her smile returned. "I might have a job."

With staff and his uncle potentially within hearing distance, he whispered, "That's great!"

She quietly replied, "Thank you. I'm pretty excited."

Then he noticed the joy shining in her blue eyes, and the oddest sensation swirled through him. Something like disappointment combined with confusion. The confusion stopped him cold. All along they'd talked about her going back to New York. They'd even made her periodically returning to Manhattan for work part of their ruse. In private, they'd discussed her business. He'd given her pointers. The last thing he should be was confused. This was their real life. He could not be sad she was talking about something she'd be doing when she left—

For good. She would never come back. They would spend Thanksgiving and Christmas together, but she'd never come back to the beach house. The realization was like a punch in the gut. His breathing froze.

Chef Alice entered the dining room carrying a plate with eggs, bacon and toast and set it in front of him before she walked to the buffet to retrieve the coffeepot. She poured him a cup then set the pot on the table so he could get refills for himself.

Dylan thanked her and she returned to the kitchen.

Lilibet laughed. "Did you phone in your order?"

"No. This is what I normally eat. If I don't tell her otherwise, Alice just makes this." He picked up a piece of toast.

Lilibet said, "When you get back from fishing maybe we could take your uncle into town for some sightseeing?"

Dylan shook his head. "He'll nap this afternoon."

"That's right."

She was working to accommodate him, trying to make up for missing this morning. Even as he fought the syrupy jolt of happiness he always got when dealing with her, he couldn't let her worry that she wasn't keeping up her end of the bargain. She'd been perfect. His uncle was happy. He was happy. Her business was showing signs of new life. She didn't have to scramble to please him.

"You don't have to feel bad about not joining us this morning. My uncle and I will be fine. I promised you we would work something out about your job in Manhattan," he said, picking up the story they'd started for the staff about why she had to go back to New York the same day they'd arrived in Belize. He caught her hand and squeezed. "I want you to be happy."

She smiled like the blushing bride she was supposed to be, and he smiled like the happy groom he was supposed to be. But though they'd done everything right, the realization that she'd be returning to Manhattan forever crept up on him again. He shoved that thought to the back of his brain because being melancholy about it was wrong and the emotion would disappear when she went home after his uncle did. Still, he didn't feel like he could hang around.

He rose. "I'm suddenly not hungry. I'm going to find Uncle Dom and get out on the water."

He kissed her again, quickly, not risking that he'd want to linger and left the dining room.

Lilibet busied herself with her bagel so she didn't have to watch him leave. No matter how much she wanted to be real with him, she couldn't. Period. He was wounded, so careful about relationships that starting something with her—no matter how attracted they seemed to be to each other—wasn't something he wanted, and she respected that. Plus, she knew not to push someone who didn't want to be pushed. She'd had a live-in lover cheat on her and move out without her even suspecting there was a problem in their relationship. This time, she wouldn't miss the cues about how he really felt. She wouldn't set herself up for another heartbreak.

Desolation tried to overwhelm her, but she had nothing to be sad about. This was a deal. She barely knew Dylan. She had a potential new client. Her life was on the upswing.

She finished breakfast, then walked into Dylan's office, took a seat on the chair in front of her computer and placed the video call, using the link Charlotte Montgomery had given her.

After exchanging pleasantries, pretty redhead Charlotte got right to the point. "I need help choosing a wedding planner. My friend told me you found one for her when her planner bailed a few days before her wedding."

"You heard about that?"

Charlotte nodded. "From Patty Finnegan. We work together. Anyway, I can't plan a wedding on my own. I'm a normal person, not high society and my husband's family is into all of that. I'm afraid my very vocal soon-to-be mother-in-law will just take over because I'm clueless."

"I'm sure you're not clueless."

"To plan a wedding in rural Ohio…not clueless. To plan something in Manhattan, I'm lost. Honestly, I need to feel the wedding planner is on my side so to speak. That's why I want help finding someone who isn't merely good, but also someone who understands it's my wedding and I want it to be my wedding."

"I see what you're saying. I'll need a few days to research and then you and I can meet in person in Manhattan. I'll bring a list of potential wedding planners. Then we'll interview the ones you like. When we find someone that you click with, we'll know we have your wedding planner."

Charlotte sighed with relief. "Yes."

"Before we go any further, you need to know the wedding planner's fee and my fee are two different things. My fee will be significantly lower. I'll charge by the hour for research, meeting with you, interviewing the wedding planners, et cetera. The wedding planner will be a lot more expensive."

Charlotte batted her hand. "I don't care. I'm willing to pay whatever the fee is, and my fiancé agrees. He wants me to have the wedding I want, not the wedding his mom wants."

Lilibet laughed, though with two parents who were always trying to guide her into law school she understood Charlotte's apprehension completely.

She and Charlotte set a time to meet in Manhattan, and she walked out into the pool area. Staring out at the ocean, she thought about how easily Dylan had accepted that she couldn't go out on the boat that morning and realized how fair Dylan was, even if he didn't see it. Losing his father, having a difficult marriage and a mom who had moved on without him, he might have erected emotional barriers, but he understood people better than he thought he did.

But that only cemented the sense that she had to watch herself around him. If he refused to take their relationship to the level that they both seemed to want, he had good reason.

And she did not want to look like a fool again.

Or get her heart broken.

At lunchtime, Dylan and his uncle returned from fishing and went directly to the pool area, looking for Lilibet. He told himself he was only scouting her out to play the part of smitten newlywed for his uncle. He would keep all other emotions out of it, not for his sanity, but in fairness to her. Because he did like her.

They stepped out onto the patio only to find it empty. He angled his hands on his hips. "Her video chat had to be over by now, but she could very well be checking her emails or working."

"I'm getting a beer. Want one?"

He faced his uncle. "No. I think I'll go check on Lilibet." He frowned. "Who knows what her potential client wanted. Maybe it was something she could research, or an email to be sent, or something she could do from her laptop. I'll be back in a minute."

He headed to the office. Two feet away from

the open door, he heard Lilibet talking. "Don't, Mom, it isn't that big of a deal—"

"Really? Going on vacation with a superstar businessman isn't a big deal?"

He stopped dead in his tracks.

"Dylan Olsen isn't just some guy you can date and expect no one to notice or care."

"Stop, Mom. Don't get ahead of yourself. We came to Belize to have enough privacy that he could help me reevaluate my business. That's all. Besides, there can't be anything between us. Dylan lives in Belize. I live in Manhattan. The logistics don't work. If you want to have lunch when I return, I can explain all the great things he's helping me to see."

Her mom sighed heavily, and Dylan chuckled. He'd told Lilibet that her dad looked like the kind of guy who would check up on them, but George McDonald had cleverly sent her mother instead. Lilibet must have taken his advice about her parents missing her because she'd offered a lunch date. Plus, she was preparing her mom for the fact that they wouldn't be together when she returned home. She really was on top of things. And—given that his uncle was out by the pool and couldn't hear any of this, and the staff were nowhere around—he could help her.

He walked into the office.

"Hey, Lilibet…" He stopped abruptly, pretending to be surprised to see her on a video call.

"Hello," he said politely. "Sorry to interrupt. I just came in to see what Lilibet wants for lunch."

Lilibet's mom couldn't contain her happiness. "No problem at all! I'm Sandy McDonald, Lilibet's mom."

"It's nice to meet you. I'm Dylan Olsen."

"I know!" she all but cooed. "My husband tells you met my daughter at university."

"My senior year. We hadn't seen each other until we ran into each other a few weeks ago."

"I'm glad you did."

He walked to Lilibet's chair and put his hands on the tall back, to be closer to the small laptop screen. "When she mentioned her business and wanting to reboot it, we came to my beach house for privacy. But—"

"Hey! Where is everybody?"

Obviously hearing Uncle Dom's voice, Lilibet spun to face him, her eyes wide.

So much for telling her mom they'd come here for privacy. "That's my uncle. Probably ready for a swim," he said quickly. "He's never around when we're working."

"I'll see you at the pool," he said to Lilibet. Then, "It was nice to meet you, Mrs. McDonald."

She batted her hand. "Sandy. Please."

"Nice to meet you, Sandy." He raced into the hall and wasn't surprised to find his uncle halfway to the office door.

"I should have known you'd try to sneak in some work."

"Nope," he said, turning his uncle around by sliding his arm across his shoulder and steering him back where he'd come from. "I found Lilibet in the office. We need to get lunch and tell Alice what we'd like for dinner."

Totally distracted away from Lilibet's call with her mom, and happily onto the subject of food, Uncle Dom said, "I'd love a salad for lunch. Something with grilled chicken and tomatoes."

Dylan glanced back toward his office. "And what about dinner?"

"If you'd caught something today, we could have had fish."

"We can still have fish."

They decided on tuna as they walked toward the door to the pool. Dylan veered off to the kitchen to talk with Alice. When he returned to the patio, his uncle had settled in a chaise lounge with his beer. Dylan dove into the water, and a couple of minutes later Lilibet came outside too.

He immediately climbed out of the pool. Keeping the conversation away from her mom, he said, "So what happened with your possible client this morning?"

She smiled broadly. "I got the job!"

"You did! That's great!"

"It's another good one. The client is having a big wedding. She's not high society but her groom is.

She's planning a society wedding and can't manage it without help. She needs me to create a list of potential wedding planners and join her when she interviews them."

"You're not simply going to pick one for her?"

"No. She needs to be able to work with the wedding planner. She needs to know whoever she chooses will understand what she wants. She couldn't let me just pick one…but she also needed someone to sift through the list of planners in Manhattan and bring it down to a manageable number. While we're interviewing them, I'll watch for things she might not notice. She's never planned a wedding before. I've been on the periphery of several."

He couldn't imagine how that was fun, but from the light in Lilibet's eyes, he realized it was fun for her. "That's great."

"It is! When I searched her name, I found that she works for a big investment firm and lives in a large condo building. There are potentially hundreds of referrals from her if I do a good job."

"What do you mean, *if* you do a good job. You'll do a great job. I've seen your dedication and commitment."

She laughed. "I don't take anything for granted."

"That's why you'll eventually succeed. You don't leave anything to chance."

Uncle Dom called from his chaise, "I still think

you're crazy to leave here to go back to Manhattan for work."

"With two private planes at her disposal, going to and from Manhattan isn't a big deal," Dylan said with a laugh.

"But why?" Uncle Dom asked, sitting up on the chaise. "It's not like you need the money."

In the three-second pause that followed, Dylan worried that Uncle Dom was still looking for marriage loopholes, then Lilibet walked over and sat on the chair beside his.

"Do you know what I do?"

His nose wrinkled. "Not really."

"I'm a problem solver. I help people."

Dylan's heart almost stopped. If his uncle was looking for loopholes, trying to figure out if this was a real marriage, she'd basically handed him an avenue to make assumptions. She was a problem solver. Dylan had had a problem…

Lord, the connection was right there!

She smiled. "My parents are lawyers, so I learned a thing or two listening to them talk about cases over dinner, but while understanding how important their job of helping people was, I don't take on anything legal. I do things like help a newly engaged woman find the right wedding planner or help a mom find a way to get her kids to school while she's out of town because her live-in nanny can't drive. There are a lot of people in

Manhattan who just need a little help. I love providing it."

Dom frowned. "Sounds like something friends used to do for each other."

Lilibet laughed. "Yes. And friends still do things like that, but sometimes people want to keep their shortcomings private. My new bride doesn't want anyone to know she doesn't have enough confidence to even choose a wedding planner. That's where I come in. No one needs know that I'm not her friend, that she hired me to help her choose a wedding planner, and she doesn't have to be embarrassed."

Dylan held his breath, waiting. His uncle was one of the smartest people he knew. If he was suspicious, he'd run this through his brain and put two and two together.

Instead, Dom patted her hand. "You're a good person Lilibet Olsen."

Dylan's shoulders softened with relief. Uncle Dom hadn't been looking for trouble. But why would he? By now, he genuinely liked Lilibet, and he saw her kindness. He'd asked why she would leave because he was concerned. Not because he was checking up on them.

Still, it was the way Uncle Dom called her Lilibet Olsen that settled in his soul like a feather gently falling to earth. Despite having a wedding ceremony, sleeping in the same bed, pretending to be married, nothing had connected him to Lilibet like his uncle calling her by their family name.

It suited her.

One of Alice's sous-chefs opened the patio door to let them know lunch was ready and they could come in to eat. Uncle Dom immediately rose, offering his hand to help Lilibet stand.

For the first time, Dylan saw what Lilibet had seen all along. The better this ruse worked, the more disappointed his uncle would be when they divorced. More than that, he would miss her. Because she was wonderful, his uncle would badger him relentlessly about what had gone wrong—

Until he realized Dylan was at fault. After all, Dylan had botched his first marriage. Or, worse, he'd think he hadn't been able to handle being married again. Which was very close to the truth. And once again, his uncle would be worried about him.

The arrangement Dylan had believed so perfect might do exactly the opposite of what he had planned.

CHAPTER ELEVEN

THAT NIGHT, DYLAN worked until well past midnight. Lilibet played the role of disappointed wife when he said he had some calls to make and would be going to his office.

She went to bed alone, glad she would be asleep before he came to bed, but as she curled into the covers, she realized this would be what she would be facing when she returned to Manhattan. She would miss him. Without even trying, she'd gotten accustomed to being around Dylan, enjoying his company, appreciating the things he'd told her about business and the advice he'd given her for her future. But she would miss his sensitivity and his ability to have fun and enjoy life more. He'd helped her sort through her career possibilities, as he reminded her that everything couldn't be about work. Knowing him had changed her.

The next day, they took Dylan's uncle into Belize City to sightsee and have lunch at the restaurant Dom had chosen for them the night he wanted them to have dinner alone. When they returned, he conked out on the chaise lounge by the pool and Dylan again went to work.

Lilibet and Dylan's communication dwindled to the way they had managed it the day they'd arrived. They didn't speak except to execute the ruse. Still, she couldn't argue with this system. She was leaving. They weren't staying married or even remaining friends. This time next week, she would be in Manhattan, living her old life—except better. She'd be leaving her condo, throwing herself fully into making her business work. And if it didn't, then she'd reevaluate. She might take a class or two that would allow her to find employment with an existing company and do her problem-solver work as a side hustle.

Agreeing to take this job had helped her in so many ways that her whole life could be different when she went home.

She slipped into a one-piece peach-colored swimsuit and spent the afternoon relaxing, thinking about her new client, getting excited about finding a less expensive apartment. When Dylan came out in his swimming trunks, she decided to do as he had done: leave him alone while his uncle slept. She went to the office to research wedding planners for Charlotte Montgomery.

But when Uncle Dom woke in the late afternoon, she returned to the pool and her assignment as Dyan's loving wife. Dom told stories of

Manhattan back in the seventies, then suggested they play rummy.

Dylan found a deck of cards, and they sat at a round table with a bright blue umbrella. Uncle Dom decided they'd play for a penny a point.

"It's been a few years since I've done this," Lilibet admitted with a wince.

"It'll come back to you," Dom said.

Dylan laughed. "My uncle is a shyster. He's trying to get all your money."

"I don't have any money," she said automatically.

Dylan looked about to panic but Uncle Dom laughed. "Your husband is good for it."

Lilibet smiled. "Okay, since I'm covered for this, penny a point it is."

About an hour into the game, Dylan went to his office for a scheduled call he couldn't get out of. A half hour after that, Dom decided to go to his room to shower. When Dylan returned he followed suit, but Lilibet walked down to the ocean to let the waves lap at her toes. She'd begun the process of deprogramming, and she wasn't going to mess with her progress. She was only here three more days. Rather than let disappointment set in, she forced herself to think of the good things: focusing on getting the word out about her business, returning her apartment to her parents, rethinking her future.

When Dylan returned to the pool, dressed in

shorts and a tropical shirt, she rose from her chair and headed inside. He gave her a strange look, as if he was ready to question her, but in the last second, he seemed to understand that Uncle Dom wouldn't see or know they'd been apart while he'd been upstairs dressing for dinner. He didn't say anything as she passed by.

They had a fun dinner with Dom telling more stories, this time about a yacht club he had belonged to when he was younger. Glad he was happy, she immersed herself in the role of being part of his family, but she suddenly became sad that she really wasn't part of Uncle Dom's family. He was a nice guy. A great guy who had taken in his nephew when Dylan's mom had moved away.

Reminded of the difficulties in Dylan's life, her heart softened a bit. She'd never met anyone to whom she was so instantly attuned. But they were in a weird, complicated situation. And her life was also about to change dramatically. She couldn't shift her plans.

They sat on the patio continuing their conversation until Dom yawned and stretched, rising as he announced, "I'm going to bed since I have an early flight in the morning."

Lilibet's gaze automatically jumped to Dylan, who obviously tried to cover his surprise with a laugh. "I thought you were staying a few more days?"

"Nope. We had fun, but I'm ready to go home."

"That's silly. At least stay the week like you said you were going to. What else have you got to do?"

"Woo a widow," he said casually, walking to the patio door. "Besides, your wife has a new client she wants to get to." He paused a few feet before he got to the door. "Actually, we could share a ride home."

Lilibet's heart stopped. She might like Uncle Dom. She might believe he'd bought the story about their marriage. But she didn't trust herself. Talking to him was so comfortable, it was disarming. It would be too easy to slip up on their long flight to Manhattan.

Dylan snorted. "You can go, but I'm not letting my new wife leave until she has to," he said, playing his role as lovesick husband. "She's already set her meeting time. No need for her to go early."

Air returned to Lilibet's lungs.

Dom laughed and went inside.

Lilibet fell against the back of her chaise lounge. "That was close."

"It was. But I think I handled it nicely."

"You did! You're getting really good at this."

He grinned. "Feel like a walk on the beach?"

There was nothing like a stroll along the water when the sun had set and the waves casually rolled to the shore. Calming and romantic.

Probably not a good idea.

"Actually, there are things we need to talk

about. A sort of debrief about the job and where we go from here."

He drew a long breath. "Maybe we should save that for after Uncle Dom leaves. You know. Just in case he's lurking around a corner."

She stifled a laugh at the picture that formed in her brain. But Dylan was right. Though Uncle Dom probably wouldn't hear them on the beach, waiting to talk until he left would ensure the conversation wouldn't be heard.

She shrugged, then stood up. For as much as she didn't believe a walk on the beach was a good idea, she also didn't want to spend time alone with Dylan on this perfect patio, feeling things she wasn't allowed to feel.

"I think I'll go upstairs and get organized. I might not be leaving with your uncle, but I'm still leaving tomorrow. I need to be ready."

He said, "Okay," but ten minutes later he joined her in the massive closet. "I know the staff is gone for the day, and Uncle Dom had left for his room, but I didn't want to jinx all our hard work by debriefing out in the open. I didn't want to ruin things on the last night when we're only about twelve hours away from declaring ourselves a success."

She laughed as she tucked a shirt into her suitcase. He really wasn't one to leave things to chance. "Good call."

He sat on the seat by a full-length mirror. "So, what time do you want to go tomorrow?"

She saw herself riding to the airport alone, climbing the three steps of his small jet, glancing back for one last look at the beautiful countryside, then ducking inside knowing she'd never return. Her heart hurt, but she smiled.

"Just to be on the safe side, I thought we should plan on noon."

She swore she saw his eyes brighten a bit, but the sudden burst of happiness quickly disappeared.

"I'll call the pilot."

He rose from the chair and left the closet. She finished packing, leaving pajamas and an outfit for the next day on the granite countertop of the island in the middle of the big room. She showered, put on the pajamas and drew a long uncertain breath.

This would be the last time they would sleep together.

She shook her head to clear it and walked into the bedroom to find Dylan already in bed.

She slid under the covers on her side. "Good night."

"Good night."

The room dripped with tension, but she quickly wondered if perhaps only she was tense. He hadn't looked at her with longing—or any sort of interest at all—since the night they'd danced. There was nothing to be nervous or concerned about. He wasn't going to make a move. They'd kissed only light, brief kisses of hello and goodbye when his uncle was around. Anything she sensed had to be all in her head.

He shifted on his pillow, then slid up and turned on the lamp. "I know we're not going to talk specifics of the job until Uncle Dom leaves. But in case we get bogged down in the business end of things in our debriefing, I need to tell you how good of a job you did."

She sat up and turned on her lamp too. "Thank you. Let's just say the week was interesting."

Dylan laughed, studying her beautiful face in the lamplight, knowing he would miss her even though that was foolish. They barely knew each other. Their lives didn't intersect personally or professionally. As she'd told her mom, she lived in Manhattan. He lived here. After Thanksgiving and Christmas, there was a chance he'd never see her again.

"Interesting is as good of a word as any."

"Your uncle is great. Your home is wonderful. I'd steal Chef Alice from you if I had the money. And you helped me think through my life. I can't thank you enough."

The fact that he had helped her filled him with pride. "No. Thank you. You made the time happy, fun. I hadn't realized how much my uncle and I needed that."

She dismissed him with a wave of her hand.

"I loved going out on the boat. I loved having so much time to relax. I don't think I've spent so long focused on fun since university. Even then, I got a little intense my last year. You and your uncle made me realize I need to change that. Do some fun things. Do some things just because I want to, not because everything has to have an endgame."

Their gazes met. Feelings he'd been fighting for days danced through him. Enjoying her company. Being part of something beyond himself or his work. Kisses that started off as playacting that turned into something more—

For him.

For her, they were a job, for which he was paying her. This week might have helped her to realize she needed more fun in her life, but that didn't necessarily mean fun with him.

He hated thinking that. Though they lived in different parts of the world and had different lives, he liked her. He wanted to believe she liked him too. Even if nothing could come of it.

It suddenly hit him that they were alone, with his uncle tucked away on the second floor. If he kissed her now, it would be because he wanted to. If she kissed him back, it would be because she wanted to.

His heart stuttered.

Seconds ticked by.

Indecision became longing, especially when he realized this might be his only opportunity to kiss her for real. They'd be with his uncle for Thanksgiving and Christmas. No alone time. If he kissed her then, it would be part of their deal.

He shifted a bit in her direction, indecision still dogging him. As it was, they were making a clean break. Their week together was nothing but a transaction. If anything was happening between them, it was hidden. As long as they didn't bring it out in the open, it wouldn't affect their deal.

But he hadn't felt like this with a woman in forever. Or maybe ever. Lilibet was so different than Janine that his emotions were also different.

Easier.

Happier.

She raised her hand to the top of the covers, and the diamond ring he'd bought for their marriage caught the light of the lamp and winked at him.

The flash of reality that hit him could have stopped his heart. The ring was a symbol of their marriage. A real marriage as declared by the state of Nevada, but a part of a business strategy. They might be alone, but they weren't out of this charade.

Disappointed, he eased down on his pillow. Regret filled him, but he ignored it. Kissing her would only confuse things. He'd had enough pain and confusion in his life to last forever. He would never deliberately put himself in a bad position again.

The next day, Lilibet awoke to an empty bed. Relief rippled through her. Crazy thoughts about their last night together had tangoed through her brain while they were talking the night before and nudged her to want to say things that were unspeakable.

Like an invitation for him to call her when he was in Manhattan. Foolish.

Or a suggestion that she could visit him in Belize again. Desperate.

Or the urge to simply kiss him. Go with action instead of words.

But common sense wouldn't let her say or do anything. Dylan was a strong, pragmatic guy. If he felt something for her, he would have said it… or kissed her. Alone in his bedroom, with no uncle to impress, a kiss would have been real. It would have spoken volumes. It would have opened doors.

But he'd done nothing. Said nothing.

She should be relieved. A kiss, a conversation about how there might be real feelings between them, would have only complicated things.

She showered then realized the clothes she'd kept out of her suitcase weren't casual enough for a morning at the beach house. After all, Uncle Dom thought she was staying after he left, living here with Dylan. She had to look the part. She reopened her bag to pull out shorts and a T-shirt.

The men were seated at the dining room table when she arrived downstairs. Chef Alice brought her a lightly toasted bagel and Dylan poured her a cup of coffee. Uncle Dom laughed at a joke he had made. It was disarmingly normal, as if this was where they all belonged, what they should be doing.

The truth of it whispered through her, reminding her that she and Dylan would be alone for several hours if she wanted to say something, to tell him she liked him and suggest they meet if he ever had business in New York.

She nixed that idea. Even if he let her down gently, he would still be letting her down.

Why risk a bruised heart when she had so much to look forward to at home? Maybe a whole new life. Or at least a whole new way to look at life.

In what felt like minutes, Dom glanced at his watch, announced it was time to go and rose.

Dylan rose too. “Let me walk you to the car.”

“I’m fine,” Uncle Dom protested.

Dylan shook his head. “Maybe I like seeing you off, making sure you get into the car okay.”

His uncle laughed. “I’m not that old.”

Lilibet joined them as they walked to the sedan. As casually and normally as any newly married man, Dylan slipped his arm around her waist, walking beside her to the car Jeremy would drive to the airstrip.

Sadness billowed through her, and she allowed it, though she continued to smile. This time her achy heart wasn’t about Dylan. She would miss Uncle Dom.

When they reached the car, she hugged him fiercely. "I will miss you."

He hugged her back. "Maybe when you are on one of your jaunts to Manhattan to help some poor soul, you could take me to lunch."

She laughed. "I would love that."

As she stepped back, Dylan hugged his uncle.

"You know, you could join your wife when she comes to Manhattan."

"It all depends on my workload. Besides, won't you be busy with your widow?"

Dom laughed. "Don't know. This is new territory for me."

"You were a Casanova. You'll sweep her off her feet."

Dom snorted. "Yeah. You're right."

Lilibet laughed, though she fought tears, the truth of the situation so obvious it hurt to admit it. She wanted this. A fun, happy relationship with a family, a family that didn't base their love of her on her success in life. A partner who loved her as simply and wonderfully as Dylan was pretending to love her.

She *wanted* it.

But she couldn't have it. Not with him. And maybe not for a few years while she straightened out her life.

Jeremy opened the back door but before Dom slid inside the car, he said, "I already called my investment guy. I set a meeting with him for Tuesday. That way I can get the ball rolling on shifting your stock back to you."

"I appreciate that."

Dom nodded. "You should come to Manhattan with Lilibet in case we need you."

"You think you will?"

"I have no idea, but it's better for you to be there than not."

Dylan laughed. "Whatever."

Dom unexpectedly hugged Dylan again. "I mean it. You could fly to Manhattan with Lilibet every once in a while."

Dylan coughed, as if holding back tears. "I will. But you know you're always welcome here. Hey, bring the widow."

Dom chuckled and slid into the back seat of the car. "I might just do that."

Lilibet and Dylan stood with their arms hooked around each other's waist as the sedan drove off the property. She would have thought Dylan would immediately step away, but he stood like that beside her for a few minutes after the car disappeared down the road.

When he finally moved away, Lilibet said, "You know, since we have a few hours, I think I'll go upstairs to change into my bathing suit so I can swim."

He gave her a funny look before he said, "That's a good idea."

She almost suggested they debrief in the room

before she changed into her bathing suit, but they'd talked the night before. He believed she'd done a good job. There wasn't much else to say except to talk about money. Plus, she had a few suggestions for the weeks before Thanksgiving and Christmas. Of course, she could give those as he walked her to the car when she left for the airstrip.

With only small items to discuss, swimming for a few hours was a way to put some distance between them, as she killed time and hopefully overrode the sadness she felt when Uncle Dom left because it was wrong. This was a job. A job that was winding down. She should not be sad. End of story.

She rode the elevator to the primary suite, walked back to the huge closet and slipped into the peach bathing suit and white lace cover-up.

When she came back to the bedroom, Dylan was waiting for her. "I thought you were talking about coming up here for our official debrief. I didn't realize you really were going to swim."

She chuckled. "So that's why you looked at me funny." He'd thought she was sending him a message. "We actually discussed most of it last night, though I have a suggestion or two for you about how to handle the next few months."

"You do?"

"Hey, I might not be with you, but your uncle still believes we're married and you have to act like it. You'll also get phone calls from your uncle.

I can't always be in the shower so you might want to tell him I flew to Manhattan for a job a few of those times. That will also work with your staff. If I'm not going to be here, they have to believe I'm on a really important job."

It struck her that she could tell him that with her never returning to Belize, he should fly to Manhattan to make it appear he'd come to New York to visit her. Or maybe he really could visit her. But she stopped herself. Technically the job was a week in Belize and two holiday dinners. He needed to be able to navigate the rest of September, October and November without her.

"Plus, telling him you're working isn't a lie."

She drew a quick breath. Pretending she was in New York for work suddenly felt like a big hole in their story. It seemed off that two people so in love they ran away and got married would spend so much time apart.

Staff would see it. Uncle Dom was too smart not to question it.

"Telling your uncle I'm in Manhattan for work isn't a lie. But it's a long stretch of time until Thanksgiving. Maybe you should fly up to Manhattan in October and November. You can visit him and tell him you're in New York because I can't be in Belize, make it sound like we're living part of the time in my condo. That way our story will be more believable. Plus, you have a great relationship with your uncle, and you need each other. It was as if this visit reminded you both of that. You might not want to lose that."

"Do you think the three of us should have lunch or something?"

"Maybe. But remember, this week was about you and your uncle reconnecting. You don't need me for that. You can have lunch alone, telling him I'm working, and keep that connection alive while you make our marriage look legit by making it appear we weren't apart for almost two months."

"Makes sense." He shook his head. "You know, I hadn't realized how disconnected my uncle and I had become until this week. You really did do a great job. And I want you to know that I'll be depositing the entire four-month fee into your account now."

"You don't have to do that."

"I do. Actually, it's easier for me this way."

The room grew silent and once again Lilibet remembered this was how it was their first day here. How the only conversation they had was to facilitate their temporary marriage. No more laughing. No more discovering things about each other. Nothing casual and easy about their dealings.

The distance between them was a weight in the room. It felt so wrong—

But she had a client to go home to and a new apartment to find. Her life was about to get infinitely better. She should not be sad.

She sucked in a breath and smiled professionally. "I appreciate it. I'll go home and pay my HOA fees and start looking for something to rent."

"Better talk to your parents first."

Just like that, the closeness she felt with him returned. He'd been so good to her parents and so easy with advice it was impossible to pretend they hadn't made a connection.

But did that matter with someone who wasn't really in her life?

"I will. I can't just move out and hand them the keys. They need to be prepared. I also wouldn't feel right taking the money for the sale of the condo. It's theirs." She pulled in another breath. "So, before I start looking for an apartment, I'll talk to them. I feel like that's the first step to starting over."

"If nothing else, it's a way to show them you can stand on your own two feet."

The room grew silent again and though Dylan longed to go to the pool and swim with her, he forced himself to walk to the elevator, to fight the feeling that he was missing out on a good thing with her. He was keeping his distance for *her*. Not for himself, not only because he was wary of relationships, but because he did not want to hurt her.

He reached the door and pressed the button for it to open, but she stopped him. "Wait."

Unexpected hope roared through him. Would

it be a whole different situation if she approached him? Made a pass at him?

But when he turned, she was pulling off the ring he'd bought her.

"Here."

Seeing the ring the night before had reminded him of their temporary marriage and stopped him from kissing her for real. Watching her take it off hit him like a boulder from out of the blue. It was a sign that this part—the fun part—of their temporary marriage was over. She really was leaving.

Still, he very calmly said, "Hold on to it. You'll need it for Thanksgiving and Christmas."

She shook her head and walked over to hand it to him. "I'd prefer you keep it. Bring it with you when you come to Manhattan for the holidays. It's too expensive for me to be holding on to it."

"Okay. I'll stash it somewhere."

"Good."

With that, she eased around him and slid into the open elevator. He didn't say anything as the door closed, and the little car headed down to the first floor.

He held the ring between his thumb and index finger, watching it glitter in the sunlight pouring into the room. Sadness followed him into the big closet and to the drawer where he kept tie clips and cuff links, things he never wore here in paradise. He nestled the ring into a holder and closed the drawer on that part of his life—until Thanksgiving.

CHAPTER TWELVE

As Dylan walked Lilibet to the car, he ignored the disappointment that dogged him. It might not be foolish to miss her. She'd helped him a great deal. But their marriage was part of a plan. They didn't have the feelings that kept creeping up on him.

Jeremy tucked her luggage into the trunk and slammed the lid closed, as they walked over to the back door of the sedan.

This was it. "I guess I'll see you."

She smiled. "Yeah."

He shoved his hands into the pockets of his jeans.

Her eyebrows rose.

He frowned, then he realized that even without his uncle being around, they were still playacting for the staff. Jeremy would expect him to kiss her goodbye, the same way the staff would expect him to go to New York, if she couldn't be here. She was always on top of things and he was glad she'd thought ahead, encouraging him to fly to New York, to pretend to be visiting her. Especially since he could easily do some business on those trips when he was supposed to be with her. He thanked God he hadn't mentioned not seeing her until Thanksgiving, then breached the step that separated them and slid his hands to her waist. His heart thudded. He'd wanted to kiss her so badly the night before and now he got to—except it wasn't the same. This was make believe.

Letting her know he'd figured things out, he said, "You can stay in Manhattan as long as you need to," as a reason for the staff when she didn't return to Belize. "I'll just hop on the jet when I miss you."

She laughed. "We'll take your uncle to lunch."

He smiled at her, his heart calling him a damned fool for not taking advantage of the opportunities he'd had the night before, but he ignored it because this was the right thing to do. Now, all he had to do was kiss her goodbye to end this part of the charade for his staff.

He lowered his head slowly as she slid her arms around his neck. He wouldn't let himself dwell on the pleasure of having her touch him. But the second his lips met hers, that mission flew out the window. Everything soft and happy about her drew him, filled him with so much emotion that he couldn't suppress his feelings. Under the guise of making the kiss believable, he let himself indulge, let himself feel every nuance of arousal and pure unadulterated joy.

Then he stepped back.

She gazed up at him, looking as starry-eyed as he felt. Time stopped. Hope mixed with warnings and reminders that this couldn't be right. Then Jeremy opened the car door.

She smiled at him, rose to her tiptoes and gave him a quick kiss on the cheek before she ducked into the back seat and Jeremy got behind the steering wheel.

The kiss on the cheek confused him. Had she kissed his cheek as a friendly gesture, a sort of goodbye from one friend to another? Or had she kissed his cheek because she couldn't help herself?

The car drove off and he headed into the house, shaking his head, asking himself why he wasn't simply glad it was over. Why was he making himself nuts over something he knew couldn't happen?

He worked for several hours, making up for taking so much time away in the days before. He ate dinner alone. Sat on the patio by himself, looking at the stars, listening to the ocean, feeling more alone than he ever had in his life.

Saturday was the same. He tried going out on the water, revving his boat to life, skipping over the wakes and waves, to stop thinking about her, but it didn't work.

Lunch tasted like sand.

He skipped dinner and sat on the darkening patio drinking Manhattans, confused, unable to dodge the question of why she'd kissed his cheek.

But that was foolish. It was one simple kiss on the cheek. Why did it bedevil him?

He tossed the rest of his Manhattan into the sink of the poolside bar and went to bed. He dreamed of her and woke the next morning groggy and a little mad. He yanked his personal phone off the bedside table and called his pilot. He was going to New York.

Sunday morning, Lilibet had a short visit with her parents wherein she explained all the things Dylan had made her realize—including the fact that if she couldn't make her business profitable, she had other options. They got quiet because they wanted both of their daughters to be part of their legacy at the law firm, but they accepted her decision.

With them being somewhat congenial, she decided she might as well tell them about returning the condo to them.

"Why would you want to return the condo? That was your graduation gift."

"True, but it was a gift you gave me to live in. The HOA fees are higher than rent in other boroughs. I just think it will be easier for me to focus on my business, if I keep things simple by renting something cheaper in one of the boroughs."

Her mother sighed. "The condo is yours. If you want to sell it, sell it. But you keep the money."

Her dad agreed. "It was a gift, Lily. Besides, the

added cash will really set you up to accomplish what you want to accomplish."

Shocked, Lilibet rose. "Thank you." Part of her wanted to argue about the money from the condo, but they were right. It had been a gift. She wasn't taking a handout. And with that money she had funds to advertise and not depend on recommendations from customers. The whole world suddenly opened to her.

Happy that things really were going to work out, she bounced out of her rideshare onto the sidewalk in front of her condo building. Right before she reached for the door, Dylan stepped out of the shadows. Confusion swamped her, then she realized he probably needed her help.

Though she wished he was at her condo building to see her because he liked her, she knew he must have something for her to do. Her heart sank. Still, she pasted a smile on her face, prepared to help with whatever he needed. "What's up?"

"I decided to go with Uncle Dom to see his business manager on Tuesday. But it's only Sunday." He shrugged. "I came two days too early. So, I have time to kill."

And he'd decided to see her?

Plus, he didn't accidentally leave Belize two days early. He was too smart for that.

Even if he had, why wasn't he playing rummy with his uncle?

Because he'd wanted to see her?

Her heart swelled at the possibility, and her eyes drank in every detail of his handsome face. Still, she told herself not to make too much of it. This was a guy who'd had every opportunity to make a pass at her if he'd wanted to. And he hadn't.

"Why not spend the time with your uncle?"

"Because I wanted to see you."

She'd hoped that was true, but he'd said it so simply, so honestly, the air in her lungs froze.

"Actually, there's a question I want to ask you."

"What's that?"

He motioned toward her building. "In private."

She took out her key card and swiped it on the lock. It buzzed, and she walked them inside the condo-building lobby. A short, quiet elevator ride took them to her floor, and she led him to the door of her home.

Once they were inside, he caught her hand and pulled her into a hug. She sank against him. She didn't realize how desperately she'd missed him until this very second. When she'd returned on Friday, she'd kept herself so busy she hadn't had time to miss him. Except at night, sleeping alone, thinking about how funny, charming and smart he was.

Which was exactly why she'd kept herself busy again on Saturday.

Their gazes met. Again, she saw nothing but raw honesty in his expression.

She smiled.

He smiled. Then he kissed her, long and hard, different from their sexy kisses when they were playacting, but every bit as intense. His tongue swirled and danced with hers, and he pulled her against him more tightly.

When he broke the kiss, he took a long breath. "Our last night together, I desperately wanted to do that."

She squeezed her eyes shut. "Me too."

"Are we wrong?"

She laughed. "I don't know. I just know sleeping with you, having you a few feet away and not being able to touch you, about drove me nuts."

He slid both of his hands to her cheeks. "Maybe we should stop thinking about it, trying to label it, trying to figure it out and just follow our instincts."

She barely had time to say, "Maybe we should," before he kissed her again. Every inch of her caught fire. Hope filled her. "This might be crazy or silly or maybe just a one-time thing, but we should investigate this."

He held her gaze intensely and said, "Agreed."

She caught his hand and led him back to the bedroom. Inside the door, he pulled her to him again and kissed her deeply, the way he had at their wedding, except this time he let his hands roam her back, her butt, her shoulders as if he couldn't get enough of her.

She understood perfectly. Her hands were moving too, touching him, feeling his arms and the back she'd seen when they were swimming or boating but really hadn't been allowed to explore.

She couldn't remember their clothes coming off, only realized when they were completely naked that they'd been undressing each other. But they were both so desperate, there was no time for wishing they'd gone slowly and savored every delicious, exposed inch. Instead, they rolled to her bed, hands still skimming, still enjoying. Then he eased away so his mouth could do what his hands had been doing.

He trailed his lips down her shoulders to her fingertips and back again before they eased down her chest and breasts to her belly and below. The intensity of it roared through her like a bolt of lightning. When he returned to kiss her, she couldn't stop her hands from reaching for him, but he stopped her. Every inch of her ached with need, yet he took his time, savoring the way she believed they should have when they undressed each other.

The pleasure-pain of it almost did her in, until he finally entered her.

Then paused, savoring again.

There was a reverence to the moment—the point when they finally had what they'd both been longing for, the point when she realized he had been worth the wait—and she hoped he felt it too.

But he moved just enough to stoke the fire, slowly reigniting the need with pleasure-pain. Her entire body tingled with wanting, but she had to be sure he felt everything she did. The intensity, the joy.

Because he was concentrating, only a slight touch of her hand against his shoulder tipped him enough that she could reverse their positions. She let her lips and tongue take the same route as his had, tasting every inch of him, reveling in his groans and sighs until he reversed their positions, tipping her the way she had tipped him and sliding inside her again.

He increased the speed of his thrusts, and everything inside her exploded. Pulling out and penetrating again, he extended her pleasure until he groaned with fulfillment and collapsed against her.

After a few seconds, he rolled away to the other pillow and flopped on it with a ragged breath. "That was everything I expected and more."

She laughed. "Yeah."

"I swear I've wanted to do that for a week."

"Since the night we got married?"

He laid his arm over his forehead. "I'd say that was the start of it."

Delighted by the admission, she laughed. "Me too."

"You realize we just consummated our marriage."

"Yeah, but we didn't really talk about getting an annulment. Divorce is fine."

He snorted.

"What was the question you wanted to ask me?"

He didn't answer right away. Finally, he quietly said, "Why'd you kiss my cheek before you left?"

"What?"

"That kiss on the cheek? It didn't seem like part of our playacting. So, did you kiss me goodbye like friends? Or was there another reason?"

She didn't have to think about it, but she nonetheless hesitated. They'd always been honest with each other, but there had been limits. This admission made her vulnerable. He would never marry again. Their relationship was going nowhere. It seemed wiser to keep her feelings to herself.

Still, it was wrong to hedge now.

She pulled in a breath. "Instinct. Impulse. Take your pick. I just wanted to kiss you for real, I think. And a cheek kiss was the only possibility at my disposal at the time."

He laughed heartily. "Boy, we put ourselves in a fine mess."

Oddly, her relationship with him was one of the few things in her life that felt right, if not downright normal. "Not really. We're adults. Adults who like each other sometimes have sex." She paused for a second. Like the kiss on the cheek, this was the only option available to them. She had to be clear about what they were doing. Otherwise, she would get hurt. "Are you not okay with this?"

"I don't want to hurt you."

She hated that she was so vulnerable that even he saw it. But being a hundred percent honest, even about their potential ending, was the way to prevent that.

"Maybe you won't hurt me. I think about things very differently than I did when I first came to Belize. Sure, you're a great guy and if things worked out between us that would be amazing. But I've finally learned that sometimes in life you have to pivot."

He sat up. "Pivot?"

"Like this... I talked to my parents this morning. I told them I had options I wanted to explore, but I wasn't ever going to law school."

"That's more like a next step, not a pivot."

"Okay. How about this? They told me that the condo had been a gift and if I sell it, I should keep the money. Rather than argue, I agreed."

He chuckled. "*That* was a pivot."

"Yeah." She scooched up on her pillow so that she was half sitting. "I figured a compromise was in order since they really seemed to accept that I won't be going to law school...ever."

"That's good, then."

She sighed and said, "Yes. It felt very much like step one in a long line of things I have to do." She took a second to savor the sense of personal triumph, then said, "So, since I've got to do some changing and be more open to things, I've decided to run my whole life that way." She met his gaze. "Not to be so serious about everything and take things as they come."

Dylan watched her face and realized she hadn't drawn this conclusion lightly. Facing all that had taken time and lots of thought. She also hadn't done it for him. She'd done it for herself. He glanced down at her ring-free hand and knew he was dealing with her. Not the problem solver he'd hired. But her. Beautiful, free-spirit Lilibet.

He rolled over and pulled her to him. "I love the way your hair smells."

She snickered. "I just bared my soul, and you tell me you like the way my hair smells?"

"Not like…love. And this is me baring my soul."

"Really?"

"I don't normally let myself be so vulnerable."

She eased her hand along the sheet. "I don't normally let myself be so forward."

"What are you talking about? You weren't forward. I seduced you."

She ran her fingernails down his chest. "Maybe we seduced each other."

Arousal rippled through him. A happy need. This wasn't sex for sex's sake. This wasn't him desperately working to keep his marriage. This was a wonderful combination of desire and happiness. Without the burden of commitment or the emptiness of his typical one-night stands.

And he wanted it. He wanted every minute she

would give him today and Monday. He wouldn't wait for this to become awkward or difficult. He would walk away on Tuesday morning happy just to know her and happy they wouldn't push things until one or the other ended up hurt.

CHAPTER THIRTEEN

THEY MADE LOVE AGAIN, this time more slowly so he could enjoy things he'd glossed over the first time. They talked some more, then Lilibet suggested French toast for lunch. It was unconventional, but that was the beauty of it.

He rolled out of bed. She followed suit. He slid into his jeans. She slipped into a pretty, frilly robe. They walked out to the kitchen of her open-floor-plan condo. She pulled a bowl from the cupboard above the dishwasher, and eggs and milk from the fridge.

"Can I help?"

She smiled at him. "This is pretty much a one-person job." She motioned to the stools by the counter. "Have a seat."

He sat. Watching her cook, he said, "This really is a great condo."

She winced. "I know. That's why it's too expensive for someone trying to get a business off the ground."

"I should buy it."

"Don't even say that."

"Why not? If I bought it, you could still live here, and your parents wouldn't have to know I own it. They'd just think you'd changed your mind about selling it."

She sighed. "I'm thinking I don't need to keep another secret from my parents."

He grimaced. "Yeah, I get that." He already had her in a temporary marriage that she never intended to discuss with them. His owning the condo would be one step too far. Plus, the condo would bind them beyond the temporary marriage. That wasn't a good idea. All this was temporary. He had to remember that.

The first two pieces of French toast were prepared quickly. She plated them and slid them onto the counter to him, along with maple syrup.

"Thanks." He poured an abundance of the syrup over them, then took a bite and groaned. "Wow. That's good."

"It's the cinnamon. Others sprinkle in a bit. I really shake with my whole heart and soul."

He laughed. "Well, it accomplishes what you want. This is great."

She made six more pieces, then sat on the stool beside his. "I'm glad you like it." She offered him the serving dish with the extras. "Have some more."

He chose two more pieces and ate them with gusto. "Want to do something this afternoon?"

He said it casually, but there were a million things he'd like to do with her in the city.

She thought for a second. "We should probably go to the Met together. That way if anything about our dating comes up in conversation with your uncle on Thanksgiving, we'll have real stories to tell."

She didn't put them together again until Thanksgiving, but that didn't surprise him. She was looking at this time together the same as he was. An interlude. An encounter. Not the start of something. Not the finish.

"Okay. How about this?" He glanced at his watch and saw they had plenty of time. "Let's go to my hotel so I can change into something suitable for a few hours at the Met and then dinner."

"I like the sound of that. Gonna take me someplace nice?"

He laughed. "It'll be hard to beat this French toast, but I think we can find something."

She laughed too, then leaned in and kissed his cheek. "Let me get dressed now. I'll only be fifteen minutes or so."

As she walked away, the cheek kiss made him smile. She was a demonstrative person. That's why she'd kissed his cheek before she left Belize. She knew she would miss him, and with limited options, she'd kissed his cheek.

He liked it. A simple, honest gesture that warmed his heart.

He glanced around, seeing a TV. Knowing football was on and suddenly so comfortable that he didn't mind being alone in her home, he called down the hall, "Take your time. There's football on TV."

She was in her room about twenty minutes before returning to her living room, looking stunning in wide-leg pants with a pretty blouse and jacket. Good for both a trip to the Met and dinner after.

"That was fast."

"Met closes earlier on Sundays. We have to get a move on."

He laughed. It would be fun to be out with her, to enjoy an afternoon with no thought of work and not a bunch of mind-consuming physical exertion on a boat or a Jet Ski to use up empty hours. He loved the things he could do living in Belize, but sometimes even he knew he kept himself too busy, not wanting to think about his past.

Happy he'd come to Manhattan, he let his guard down even more. They both knew this wasn't forever. He could relax and enjoy it.

They caught a cab to his hotel, happily chatting about people on the street. Lilibet didn't gape at the opulence of the lobby of his expensive hotel. She'd been to places like this with her parents, but with chandeliers, mirrors and modern sofas, the lobby was striking. They took the elevator to his floor and walked down the silent hall to his suite. The gorgeous sitting room filled with sage green furniture, polished end tables and a bar, dripped luxury.

He said, "I'll just be a minute."

"You can have about twenty. Shower quickly."

He laughed and spontaneously kissed her, surprising her. Not that she didn't think he liked her enough to kiss her or that he wasn't romantic. It was more that he was so happy. As easygoing as he'd been on the boat or by the pool.

She told herself not to make anything of it. She liked that he was relaxed with her. But that was as far as this would go. She had work to do on her business and her life. He was wounded enough that he'd entered a fake marriage because he knew he would never marry again for real. What they both needed was simply to enjoy the afternoon.

He took less time to get dressed than she had, and he looked fabulous in simple trousers with a white shirt, no tie and a suit jacket. Considering that they would be eating together, out after dark in New York, the jacket was important.

He gave her a quick kiss again before they headed out to the street. Another cab ride took them to the Metropolitan Museum of Art. She picked up a map on the way in, but he shook his head.

"I've been here enough that I can be your tour guide."

"Okay." She set the map down and linked her arm with his. "What are you going to show me?"

"I thought we'd stroll and enjoy whatever is in our path."

She laughed, looking around at the neoclassical lobby with columns and high arches. It managed to be formal and elegant without being stuffy, as artistic as the works they were about to view. It filled her with a sense of wonder and joy. For the first time in a long time, she relaxed and let go. Even her conversation with her parents that morning disappeared from her brain.

"We're going to stroll through five thousand pieces of art?"

"Strolling means we're allowed to pause. We don't have enough time to take in everything, so we'll enjoy what we get to."

"Okay, then."

They took their time on the first floor, and she realized he really didn't want to rush, suggesting he needed the quiet afternoon. She put it all together—his coming to talk business with his uncle, his coming to her condo, his wanting to stroll—and she wondered. Had he overdone work after she and his uncle had returned home? Had the sudden quiet of his house gotten to him? Or had he been lonely?

"So, what have you been doing since your uncle and I left you on Friday?"

"Working."

"No boat breaks?"

"One, but that was it."

"On Saturday?"

"Yeah. Actually, I have something big coming up the end of next week. I'm glad we can get the return of my stock rolling on Tuesday so I can forget that and focus on the other thing."

"Interesting."

He glanced at her. "Really?"

"Yes!"

"Is that your way of telling me you want to hear more?"

"I did notice that you never talk in specifics when you mention your work. Not that it's any of my business. It just strikes me as odd that you're secretive."

"Not secretive. It's how I can separate work and my personal life. That way I'm able to set it aside at the end of the day—or for a weekend—to have a private life."

She considered that. "It does make a weird kind of sense."

"It makes perfect sense. Especially if I dedicate a certain number of hours to work and a certain amount of time to having fun."

The problem solver in her couldn't help seeing how deliberate and overplanned that was. But she also knew his history. He'd lost his wife. Before that, his father had died. His mother had walked away from him. He'd suffered three great personal losses and survived because he was a thinker, a planner. Somewhere along the way, his busy brain had decided that structure would prevent him from succumbing to the pain. Structure served him well.

Truth be told, he was helping her to realize she needed a little more structure in her life. Depending on word-of-mouth referrals to build her business was lax at best. She might have to take a course or two in advertising and marketing to figure out how to get more clients. But dedicating a certain amount of time to her business, and the rest to having a real personal life would give her balance.

He was right, but she worried that in his case he'd taken it too far. Still, it wasn't any of her business. Just a sort of red flag that would bother her if she thought this relationship was going anywhere.

They spent Monday in Central Park and her bed. Two happy people enjoying life. On Tuesday morning, they showered together, but he immediately became businessman Dylan again.

He dressed quickly, efficiently, wearing a dark suit, white shirt and tie. She was about to put on sweatpants and a T-shirt but remembering her thoughts about being more businesslike during business hours, she switched to nice pants and a sweater. She would investigate what courses she would need to take to create an overall marketing strategy, including advertising and maybe call a real estate agent about selling her condo.

She offered to make him breakfast, but he shrugged that off. "I need to get going. Plus, Uncle Dom might want breakfast." He kissed her quickly. "I'll play it by ear."

"Tell him I said hello."

"I will."

He headed to the door, and she followed him. He turned for one last goodbye.

She straightened his tie, which wasn't untidy. She simply liked the intimacy of touching him. "This was fun. Thank you."

He kissed her, a very thorough goodbye kiss as if he were storing up a memory for when he was alone in Belize. "Thank *you.* I can't remember spending a better weekend in New York."

She nervously straightened the collar of his shirt, so tempted to ask him to stay another night that she needed the continued distraction. "New York can be just as much fun as Belize."

"Yeah, but you have to wear more clothes." He sucked in a breath. "I better go. Uncle Dom will be waiting."

Her heart hurt at the thought of him leaving. She longed for just a couple more hours before they had to jump back into real life. "I could go with you...especially if you're getting breakfast."

"No. I'm going to tell him you're with your parents." He grinned. "But I'm also going to tell him that I wanted to get his opinion of you."

She lightly swatted him. "Why would you do that?"

"For fun."

"You have an odd idea of what fun is."

His expression shifted from devilish to serious. "I had to work hard to learn how to get some fun into my life. It didn't just happen naturally for me. And I'm holding on to it with both hands."

She sighed. "I know. I'm working on getting some fun into my life too, even as I set up some kind of structure for my work life, so I understand what you did."

"Okay, then." He kissed her again. "I'll see you Thanksgiving morning."

She smiled and nodded, but a little part of her soul sank with disappointment. She'd love to see him again next weekend, the weekend after, or *any* day in October or November before Thanksgiving, but her longing wasn't as significant as what he was subtly telling her. This had been a moment stolen out of time for them. Nothing permanent.

She understood why. First, they were still married as part of a business deal. That made even contemplating a real relationship complicated. Second, they lived far away from each other. She couldn't leave her life for him. Hell, she didn't even really know what her life was supposed to be like yet. She couldn't walk away for a man. Third, he couldn't leave Belize for her.

She shook her head. Why was she thinking these things? They'd had fun. Real fun. She couldn't mess that up with thoughts of permanency that couldn't happen.

Shouldn't happen. They were wrong for each other.

Sadness at the truth of that tried to rise in her soul. Stubbornly, she wouldn't let it. Yes, she recognized that she was more of a free spirit and he was a planner. It didn't really matter until she reminded herself that he was a planner because he was wounded and she was a free spirit because her life growing up had been restricted and boring.

If she and Dylan took this one step further than what they had, one of them would be hurt. And while she'd been positive it was herself she was protecting, maybe he was the one who needed protection. His peace had been hard-won. She couldn't mess with that.

Still, she struggled with closing the door as he walked away.

Why did she like him so much when they didn't fit? Their lives didn't mesh. They could not have anything real or permanent.

CHAPTER FOURTEEN

DYLAN WALKED DOWN the hall to the elevator on his way to see his uncle, happier than he'd ever been. They'd had a great time, two days of fun. They'd enjoyed themselves, but he hadn't made promises and she hadn't asked for any. They'd been just two people having fun.

Now, rested, happy, he could deal with his uncle and his stock and return to normal. In Belize. Where he belonged.

But at the end of the morning with his uncle, he stood outside his hotel and debated going inside. It was early enough that he could see Lilibet again, but he'd already violated his no-spur-of-the-moment, impulsive decisions policy by going to see her at all. He was lucky they'd had such a great time, and it had ended amicably.

Did he really want to mess with that?

Half of him eagerly said, "Yes." But the other half, the half that had kept him sane, told him that if he didn't want to give Lilibet the wrong idea, which might eventually hurt her, he should call his pilot and go home.

The half that longed to see her again wilted with disappointment, but he pulled his phone from his jacket pocket anyway and hit the screen to contact his pilot as he entered the hotel then rode the elevator to his room to get his luggage.

He spent the next two weeks being unexpectedly annoyed with his logical self for nudging him to leave New York and return to Belize without seeing Lilibet one more time. Even burying himself in work he couldn't shake the feeling. He could, however, ignore it for extended periods of time. His longings didn't matter. His sanity did. Not building up Lilibet's expectations and eventually hurting her did.

The following Monday night, he was on his patio, reading by the pool, when his phone rang. He picked it up absently, then took his gaze off his novel to check caller ID.

Uncle Dom.

He answered with a chuckle. "What's up?"

"I'm coming down again."

Dylan sat up. "What?"

"I met June—"

"June?"

"The widow in my building."

"Oh."

"And she's great." His voice dropped conspiratorially. "And she likes me."

Dylan snorted. "So why are you coming here? Running away from her? Hiding?"

"Are you kidding? Things couldn't be better. I adore June Bug, and I want her to meet you and Lilibet."

Dylan had to stifle a laugh at the nickname his uncle had already given his new friend, and told himself to stay focused on the conversation. He and Lilibet were still married. Uncle Dom liked them being married. He needed more details of his planned trip to know how to handle this.

"So, you're visiting and you're bringing June with you?"

"Yes! Pay attention!"

Dylan stopped another laugh, as his mind started calculating. He could tell his uncle and "June Bug" that Lilibet was in Manhattan working, but that excuse felt thin. It could make his whole marriage story questionable. Even if it was okay to begin easing himself toward the divorce story, he didn't want to disappoint his uncle so soon after the stock transfer.

Still talking, Uncle Dom happily said, "I think Lilibet is going to love her."

His uncle clearly wanted Lilibet in on the meeting with his new lady friend. It wasn't time to even hint that the marriage was in trouble and heading toward divorce—

The only choice was to call Lilibet and bring her to Belize to continue the ruse.

His heart happily jolted, and his spirits lifted. He wanted to see her. But he told himself not to go overboard. They'd left things in a good place. She'd seemed to understand that their time in New York together was a one-time thing. He didn't want to wreck that.

Of course, with both understanding that anything between them was temporary and that they lived in different parts of the world, neither one would go overboard with expectations—

Would they?

Uncle Dom continued talking. "God knows I love her. She's everything I didn't even realize I wanted back when I was a footloose bachelor."

That got his attention. "You *love* June already?"

"Wait till you meet her. You'll see why."

"Uncle Dom, do I need to remind you that it's only been two weeks? You're a very wealthy person and she could be...well, seeing dollar signs."

"Nope. She has her own money."

"She does?"

Dom laughed. "You're so suspicious. June is gorgeous, well off, happy to be with me. I'm telling you, she is perfect, and you have to meet her."

His suspicions dimmed but didn't totally disappear. He did need to meet this woman and make the proper assessment that his starry-eyed uncle might not be able to make. Still, he wouldn't tell Uncle Dom that.

Instead, he enthusiastically said, "Well, bring her down. Lilibet and I can't wait to meet her."

"How about Wednesday morning?"

"Sounds great."

They disconnected the call and Dylan immediately called Lilibet. He didn't let himself think of the consequences of spending more time with her. He had sorted that out. She was in the process of figuring out her life, finding herself. She didn't want a commitment. He'd given up commitments long ago. He didn't have to worry about getting too attached.

They'd be fine.

No. They'd have fun.

He could also use an unbiased person to help assess the widow June.

For thirty seconds, he considered that he was worrying about his uncle for nothing. But he couldn't just merrily accept the situation. Not that he'd interfere, but he wouldn't hesitate to investigate if he saw any red flags.

That's what he had to focus on when he called Lilibet: getting her help assessing the widow June.

Not how happy he would be to see her again.

Lilibet was already in bed when her phone rang, yanking her out of a light sleep. She grabbed it and answered. "Hello?"

"Did I wake you?"

"Dylan?"

"Yeah."

"What time is it?"

"About ten. Uncle Dom is bringing the widow

down to meet us Wednesday morning then staying through the weekend. Her name is June. He calls her June Bug. It's the funniest thing."

The easy way he talked to her went straight to her heart. She wouldn't let herself admit how much she'd missed him in the past two weeks. But she had missed him frequently enough that she was lucky he lived far away so she wasn't tempted to see him.

Their lives were too complicated for them to consider anything more than those lovely two days they'd spent together.

"I can tell them you're in Manhattan working, but I'd love for you to come to the beach house."

Her heart flipped over in her chest, but she told herself to settle down. This was the job for which she was getting paid extremely handsomely. The two days they'd spent together had to be a one-time thing.

"Uncle Dom is so excited about us meeting her that I knew you had to be here when they arrive."

"What time should I be at the airstrip?"

"Six."

"Six it is."

"I'm not dragging you away from work, am I?"

"I got Charlotte settled in with her wedding planner. She calls me once or twice a week to talk things through, but I can take those calls in your office."

"Then we're good?"

She thought so. She had her head on straight about their relationship. It was a nonstarter. They'd had fun. Released their sexual tension. But they weren't right for each other. Now, she had to fulfill her responsibilities to him.

"We're good."

"I'll see you Wednesday."

Wide awake, she rolled out of bed. She longed to let herself be excited about seeing Dylan again, but she was smarter than that. The day they'd met to talk about this job he'd told her he couldn't get married for real because his first marriage was a disaster. She'd believed him. But as they'd gotten to know each other, he'd expanded on that to include serious relationships. She believed that too. He was wounded, but he'd made a great life for himself. A safe life for himself. She respected that.

She'd been hurt by Ben because she hadn't seen the relationship for what it was. She owned the condo he lived in. When his feelings for her changed, he couldn't leave without being homeless. God only knew how long he'd pretended to still have feelings for her and God only knew how she'd missed the signs. And there had to have been signs. This time she would not let herself gloss over things that were obvious. She would admit them, face them. No more wishful thinking. She would see the truth.

When she deplaned on Wednesday morning, Libet was surprised to see Dylan leaning against a simple black sedan. Wearing shorts and a T-shirt and flip-flops, with his arms crossed on his chest, he looked comfortable and happy.

As she walked over to the car, Jeremy strode past her with her luggage, which he stowed in the trunk.

When she got close enough, Dylan said, "Hey."

She smiled. "Hey."

With Jeremy right beside the car, she knew they had to immediately fall into the role of happy husband and wife. Especially since she hadn't been around for over two weeks. Their cover story had been that she had clients, but two weeks was a long time for newlyweds to be apart. They were going to have to make this reunion count.

As expected, Dylan caught her arms and pulled her to him. Though she told herself to think of this as nothing more than the kind of kisses they'd shared initially—at their wedding and saying goodbye when she had to leave after her first trip here—she began to think of their happy time at the Met, spending hours in bed, kissing goodbye for real when he left her condo.

Joy exploded inside her, along with arousal so intense that it weakened her knees. She couldn't have said how long the kiss lasted. She also didn't care. Nothing might come of this, but she could still enjoy the moment.

He pulled away. "I missed you."

No playacting required, she said, "I missed you too."

Jeremy grinned and winked at her before he opened the car door. He'd barely shown any emotion the other times she'd been here, but today he was happy to see her. As if he were confirming that his boss had missed her.

They slid inside the vehicle. Happiness almost made her giddy, but when Dylan asked her about her work, it reminded her that the staff noticing that he had missed her shouldn't matter to her. They were playing the role that they were married. She couldn't let her real feelings slip in, though there was enough crossover in the joy she had at being here with him, and the happiness she was supposed to have at seeing her husband again after over two weeks away from each other that her behavior fit.

"So how was your time away?"

She considered all the things she'd done in the almost three weeks she'd been away and smiled at Dylan. "Charlotte's happy as a clam. Planning the wedding of the century, only needing a few confidence builder conversations every now and again. I'm helping a new client, Courtney, find a tutor. Her parents' expectations are high, and her first few weeks at university left her head spinning."

He frowned. "She couldn't find a tutor on her own?"

They'd sat close, perpetuating the marriage

myth, and the scent of him surrounded her. "Finding a tutor has to be on the down-low. Her dad's a professor. We had to find a guy willing to pretend they're dating."

Dylan laughed, catching her gaze, his brown eyes dancing. "Are you kidding?"

The humor of the similarities between Courtney's situation and their pretending to be happily married was funny. Still, she could tell he was glad to see her. That was real. She could see it in his dark, smiling eyes.

The lines between keeping up their marriage story and her real attraction to him blurred again. It was just so wonderful to see him.

She swallowed hard, reminding herself of the potential hazards of letting her genuine emotions take control. If she allowed herself to go too far for too long, she could end up hurt. Or hurting him. Disrupting the perfect life that kept him sane.

She pulled back her real emotions, dismissed all the things she had noticed, and forced herself into the role of wife who'd missed her husband, the pretend woman. Not the real Lilibet.

"Parents put a lot of pressure on kids these days. Especially parents with money. Courtney's a great girl. She wants a good education and to find a fulfilling job. She's doing this for herself as much as for them."

He grew serious. "The bottom line, though, is

that she doesn't want to disappoint them—or she wouldn't have to hide that she's hiring a tutor."

Who knew his serious voice would set her heart fluttering? The way he paid attention, really was interested in her life, always drew her to him. But this was different. After their first week together, she knew he wasn't pretending to be a nice guy. He *was* a nice guy. Who liked her and helped her and made her laugh.

Now she could add drove her crazy with desire.

Longing poured through her, but she ignored it because there were too many variables to trust it. She'd been in a relationship that she thought was real but wasn't. When someone flat out told her he wasn't interested in anything permanent or serious, she had to believe him.

"Actually, she doesn't want her parents messing in her life. If they discover she's floundering, they'll have all kinds of suggestions and input. And what they'll do is confuse the issue. Honestly, she's smart enough that I think once a tutor helps her navigate a class or two, she'll be fine."

"So, you're kind of like a big sister to this girl?"

She thought about it. "Yes."

He squeezed her hand. "I think that's what I like about you the most. You do this from your heart. You don't just find answers to problems. You have the best interest of the client as the real goal."

He couldn't have said anything more romantic to her, though there was nothing romantic about it. Except that he knew she was searching for herself, and at times like these, he showed her that things she did had value.

They continued chatting on the way to his beach house. When they arrived, Jeremy immediately took care of her bags. They also headed to the third floor, taking the stairs while Jeremy took her luggage in the elevator.

On the second-floor landing, Dylan pointed down the hall at one of four doors. "That's Uncle Dom's room. But just in case, I'll tell him that June can have the room across the hall." He ran his hand along the back of his neck. "I hope that's the right way to deal with this."

She laughed. "Let them know both rooms are available, and they'll figure out the rest."

He rolled his eyes. "That's the plan. The last thing I want to do is hear about my uncle's love life."

They finished the final set of steps to the third floor and heard the elevator leaving. A quick trip to the closet showed her that Jeremy had left her luggage by the bench. She considered unpacking, but decided she'd rather be casual and comfortable on the patio when Uncle Dom arrived.

When she turned to walk out of the room, Dylan was right behind her. So close, she almost bumped into him.

He caught her shoulders, she thought, to keep her from teetering. Instead, he yanked her to him and kissed her. She should have been shocked, but the sensuality of it melted her bones and lit her insides on fire. She wrapped her arms around him, and he lifted her off the floor, hooking her legs around his hips as he carried her to the bed. They rolled over the white comforter together, hands greedily moving along skin shivering with need.

Part of her sounded out a warning—they'd more or less agreed that spending two days together in New York was a once-in-a-lifetime thing. She ignored the reminder. Telling herself this was another one of those moments stolen out of time, she relieved him of his shirt and smoothed her hands down his solid chest. Giving in to their attraction meant nothing more than an acknowledgment that a red-hot desire flowed between them, and they should enjoy it while they could.

He unbuttoned her blouse and tossed it across the room before he undid the snap of her shorts. She didn't give him a chance to remove her panties or bra. Needing to even the score, she got rid of his shorts.

When they were finally naked, he kissed her deeply. Her breasts met his chest, and the air suddenly became difficult to breathe. She sucked in a long draft of it before he deepened the kiss. Running his hands down her sides, he groaned with pleasure.

She didn't care to have a rational thought, but the knowledge that this wouldn't last forever made her greedy. But Dylan suddenly slowed things down. The kisses he rained on her shoulders and chest had an unexpected reverence to them.

Her whole body stilled as if caught in a magical spell that connected them on a level she'd never experienced before. This meant something to him. More than an appreciation of their attraction, the way he made love to her spoke of an awareness of how special and unusual their link was.

Happiness and yearning combined into an emotion so pure she barely caught it before it trembled out of reach. But, if only for a fleeting second, she'd felt something more than desire, then physical needs overcame wistful wishes. She held her breath to savor the pleasure of him entering her and let herself fall into the delicious buildup of need and the sensual satisfaction that tiptoed along her nerve endings.

The sensuality and emotion of it nearly did Dylan in, but he held back on the emotion. Passion was one thing. Connection was even okay. It was the next step that he stopped. Even though everything inside him wanted to tumble over the edge and let himself admit what they had was worth a risk, he knew better.

Lilibet seemed to pick up on his hesitation. Rolling to her pillow, she took a long, life-sustaining breath. "I'm guessing you missed me more than you said."

He laughed with delight. "Having your own beach house away from everybody and everything is amazing…but then one day you realize just how far away you are from everybody and everything."

She laughed. "It's like good news bad news. Have you ever thought of looking beyond this beach house and making some friends down here?"

"Oh, God no. I seriously came here for peace and privacy. I can work better here than anywhere." So why had the past two weeks been so hard? Because he'd missed her?

That was the line he didn't want to cross. The admission he didn't want to make. Yes. He could say that he'd missed her the same way a normal person missed a friend, but when you combined the passion and the connection he felt with her to the longing to be around her all the time, that was the danger zone.

He rolled over and eased out of bed. "Let's surprise Uncle Dom by picking him up at the airstrip. No Jeremy. I'll drive."

"It *was* sort of nice to have you meet me."

He hadn't been able to hold himself back, and he now recognized the problem in that. Not just that he'd been so eager to see her but that she understood the significance of him coming to the airstrip.

Picking up his uncle minimized the impact of that—

For her. He still saw it. He still understood why

he had gone to the airport and what it had meant. While he didn't want her to look more deeply into it than she already had, he knew this meant he had to work on keeping those lines and boundaries in place.

Or he'd hurt her.

Or he'd get hurt.

After his uncle's plane taxied to the small hangar, Dylan pushed off the sedan's bumper and walked over to help the pilots carry the luggage to the car. The small stairway descended and a tall, slender blonde in sunglasses walked down.

Dylan joined Lilibet as she approached the jet and Uncle Dom navigated the stairs, beaming like a pirate.

Sliding his arm around the blonde, he said, "Dylan, Lilibet, this is June Simons."

Dylan stretched out his hand to shake hers. "It's nice to meet you."

Lilibet also shook her hand. "Lovely to meet you."

June slid her big sunglasses off her face. "Speaking of lovely." She glanced around. "This is beautiful."

"And it's always warm," Uncle Dom said. "Though I don't have to sell the place." He turned and hugged Dylan. "What are you doing here, picking us up? That big staff of yours go on strike?"

The trip to retrieve his uncle had been about neutralizing the way he'd been unable to stop himself from picking up Lilibet. Still, the week he and Uncle Dom had spent with Lilibet had taught him how distant he and his uncle had become, and he never wanted that to happen again.

"Staff is fine." He gave his uncle another quick squeeze and spoke honestly to keep their connection alive. He couldn't be this real with Lilibet, but he could with his uncle. "I just missed you and wanted to see you."

His uncle's face shone with pleasure, but he batted a hand. "You could see me any time you wanted to. All you have to do is fly to Manhattan with that wife of yours." He turned to Lilibet and hugged her. "And you could take me to lunch every now and again when you're in town."

Lilibet laughed. "Or you could take me. I'll bet you have a lot more money than I do."

Dom snorted. "Your husband has tons more than me. You buy."

She laughed again and linked her arm through Dom's then June's, leading them to the sedan.

Dylan could have hugged her for how well she always played her part. He knew that having a true personal relationship was making the marriage ruse easier for them both, but that added to his fears about how much he longed to be close to her. Still, he pragmatically looked to the future. Thanksgiving was now only a bit over a month away. Christmas was a month after that…then it was over. Yes, it would be difficult to explain to his uncle, but that wasn't today's problem. Today, they needed to check out pretty June. She seemed lovely, but Dylan wanted to be sure.

They chitchatted about the weather and the countryside during the half hour drive to the house. When they reached it, June's reaction was close to Lilibet's when she saw it.

"It's huge!"

Lilibet laughed. "I know. New Yorkers are always impressed by space."

Jeremy walked out of the house to the back of the car to get the bags out of the trunk.

Lilibet said, "I'll be happy to show you to your room."

Uncle Dom shook his head. "No need. I know the way. I always stay in the same room. June and I will be happy there."

June and Dom followed Jeremy into the house. When the door closed behind them, Lilibet turned to Dylan. "I guess you have the answer to your uncle's sex life."

He groaned.

"Of course, we could be interpreting this all wrong. Maybe they just cuddle."

He groaned again. "I do not want that image in my head."

"Yeah, me neither." She tucked her hand at his elbow. "Let's go make martinis. We'll loosen them up with liquor and see whose true colors come out."

"You are devious."

"We only have a few days. We can't waste time."

CHAPTER FIFTEEN

WHEN DOM AND June finally made it to the patio, Dylan and Lilibet were comfortably seated on two lounge chairs by the pool. Dylan rose. "I made martinis."

June said, "Oh, I love martinis!"

Point in her favor. Walking to the outdoor bar, he said, "I've spoken to the chef about dinner. I was thinking of Italian tonight. Chef Alice makes a wonderful lasagna."

"You'll love it," Uncle Dom said.

Dylan poured two drinks and handed them to his uncle and June. "If not, I can change the menu."

June took her martini. "Are you kidding? I love lasagna."

Dylan returned to his chaise beside Lilibet. The urge to take her hand rumbled through him, but he shook his head to clear it. They were doing well enough as a married couple. He didn't need to add to it. But the feeling didn't go away. He simply wanted to hold her hand. Unfortunately, it was the simplicity of gesture that made it wrong.

Getting them back on track, Dylan said, "We'd love to hear about you, June."

Uncle Dom groaned. "Don't be poking at her private life."

June said, "It's fine. This is family. They are curious. And I'm happy to tell them." She smiled at Dylan and Lilibet. "My husband died a little over five years ago. We'd raised three kids together. Boys. He passed right after our youngest son's wedding. It was hard."

Lilibet said, "I'm so sorry."

"It's been long enough that I've adjusted," June said pragmatically. "Taught me some good lessons though. Like live for today. But more than that, I think losing Henry taught me to just plain live. Lots of people get old and stay in their condo except for a trip to the park once a week. I like being out. Being part of my kids' lives." She laughed. "I was a boy mom and now I'm grandmother to five girls."

Dylan winced. "Five girls!"

"Grandchildren are one of life's greatest blessings. I adore them," she said. "I'm becoming a real pro at throwing tea parties."

"Been to one or two," Uncle Dom said. "June Bug gets out the real china and flavored teas. The girls love it."

Dylan sat back. June was bringing out an entirely new side of his uncle. In a way it was adorable. In another way it sent confusing feelings shooting through him. His uncle's happiness warmed his heart, but his uncle was one of those people who stayed in his condo and went to the park once a week. He hoped this change was good for him. He hoped June didn't hurt him. Didn't build expectations and then move on or move away to be with her family.

"Do your sons live in Manhattan?"

"One does. But Billy and his wife live in Ohio, and Finn and his family are in Minnesota. They're both investment counselors. New York might be a financial capital, but there are people all over the country who need help investing."

Lilibet frowned. "Why Ohio and Minnesota?"

"That's where their wives grew up."

"So, they stayed near family?"

"Met their wives at university, got married and moved close to be with their wives' families. But I now have lots of places to visit."

Lilibet laughed at that, but Dylan mulled it over. He hated being such a killjoy, but this was his uncle, the one person who'd consistently loved him and taken care of him. He would return the favor.

Dinner was light and happy with June being a good conversationalist. Dylan paid close attention to everything she said, looking for red flags. He didn't find any, but he couldn't shake his fears.

Afterward, June and Dom took a walk on the beach. Lilibet and Dylan headed outside to sit by the pool. As she lowered herself to a chair, Lilibet said, "I think she's wonderful."

"You work with a lot of people, get personal with a lot of people, so I'm hoping your opinion is worth more than mine."

"You don't like her?"

"I'm just suspicious."

"That's your nature."

He frowned. "It is?"

"Of course. You investigate investments. You troubleshoot the companies you run. You told me you read reports looking for problems. It's what you do." She reached out and caught his hand. "Relax. All my instincts about her are good. Plus, she comes with built-in grandkids. Being a bachelor your uncle didn't have any. Now he can borrow hers."

Dylan laughed and shook his head.

"It's not like they are getting married. They are dating. Let him have fun. Keep your eyes open, but don't interfere unless something actually happens.

He took a breath. "You're right."

"Of course I'm right. I'm a problem solver."

He snorted. "I'm starting to wonder if you don't just like butting into other people's business."

She raised her hands. "Who knows? That might be it. But as your uncle hinted, a lot of what I do is just what friends do for each other."

"True."

"And we're friends."

He nodded and agreed. "We're friends."

All his worries about tipping over into something else disappeared. Not because the possibility hadn't existed but because Lilibet, free spirit though she was, had a good head on her shoulders. She knew there were limits. She wouldn't let things go any further than they could manage.

The following morning, they took the boat out. June loved it and, like Lilibet, let Uncle Dom teach her to fish. They took Dylan and Lilibet to dinner the last evening of their stay and sat on the patio talking for hours. Not merely seeking information about June, all of them joined in the conversation. Dylan talked about managing the four software companies he founded. Dom talked about living in the city. Lilibet had a story or two about being a bridesmaid to six of her friends.

Dylan had to hold back a laugh. She'd said she'd been on the periphery of a few weddings. Now he knew it was six. Six weddings. It was no wonder she knew how to help panicked brides find wedding planners and deal with potential in-laws.

When the conversation died down, Uncle Dom rose from his chair and June followed suit. "We're leaving early so we need to head upstairs, but I wanted to thank you again for having us."

Dylan rose too. "It was our pleasure. We love having you here."

"And I like feeling like family again," Dom

said, glancing around the darkening patio. "I've missed us being together."

Dylan impulsively hugged him. "Me too."

"The next time Lilibet jets off to Manhattan, you come with her. But you buy dinner this time."

Dylan laughed. "I'll do that."

June and Dom said good-night and headed upstairs. The subtle lap of the ocean against the shore filled the quiet.

Lilibet broke the silence. "This whole situation worked out a lot better than you'd hoped it would."

"Yeah. It did. And Uncle Dom and I have you to thank for that."

"I just gave you an excuse to see each other."

He laughed. "I think you were too damn pretty for him to pass up the opportunity to meet you."

She shook her head. "Whatever. You two did the hard work by talking, being honest. I was proud of you both."

He sniffed and held out his hand to her. "Let's go to bed."

She lifted herself from her chair, and they walked hand in hand to the elevator and rode it to his room.

They got ready for bed casually, easily, both in the dressing room at the same time. Done with the talk of getting their stories straight and reminders of how to behave the next day, they were just two people comfortable in the easy silence.

In the bedroom, Dylan picked up the corner of

the comforter and paused. "What do you say we turn on the air-conditioning?"

Lilibet slid under the covers. "The open doors keep the room cool enough."

"Yeah, but if we close the door and turn on the air-conditioning to say, sixty-two, we can cuddle."

She stared at him blankly, then realization dawned for her and she laughed. "You want to re-create our wedding night?"

"With a much better outcome."

Happiness lit her pretty blue eyes. "Sounds romantic."

"It will be."

He walked to the thermostat and lowered the temperature, then he closed the sliding glass doors.

It took a few minutes for the room to cool, but by then they were already cuddling. She yawned. "Sorry."

"Don't be. If you're tired, go to sleep."

She hesitated.

He said, "Sleep. I'm serious."

She closed her eyes and in seconds he knew she was out cold. He kissed the top of her head, closed his eyes and fell asleep with her.

Lilibet slept blissfully, in the cold room with his warm body wrapped around her. She woke to him nibbling at her neck. A glance at the bedside clock told her it was almost six. His wake-up time.

"Did you sleep at all?"

"Of course, but I always wake at six."

"It's not quite six."

He ran his tongue along her sensitive skin. The shivers that tumbled down her spine had nothing to do with the cold.

She turned in his arms to kiss him and her pajamas and his sleep shorts were soon at the foot of the bed.

They made love, starting the day as two people so accustomed to each other the pleasure came naturally. Warmth enveloped her, along with the kind of contentment that shocked her.

This was what people searched for. This was what lovers sacrificed for, what built lives of happiness. Long marriages. Families. A story worth telling grandkids.

This was it. Not merely love but love worth finding.

Dylan's phone suddenly rang—the phone for which only twelve people had the number. He grabbed it, read the caller ID and answered. "Hey, Uncle Dom."

He sat up. "You're leaving now?" He hit the button to activate the speaker.

"Yes. We're up. We're dressed. We've eaten breakfast."

"What time did you get up? Four?"

Dom laughed. "Around there. Look, we don't want to disturb you. We just wanted to let you know we were leaving."

Dylan rolled out of bed. "We'll be right down."

"No need—"

"Yes. There is a need. We want to say goodbye."

Dylan disconnected the call and said, "Dress quickly."

She chuckled but dashed out from under the covers and into the bathroom and dressing room. She quickly slid into shorts and a T-shirt and met him in the bedroom where he was pulling a golf shirt over his head.

They rode downstairs in the elevator together. The doors opened and there stood Uncle Dom and June Bug.

Uncle Dom hugged Lilibet, then as he reached for Dylan, June hugged Lilibet.

"We've gotta get going."

Dylan frowned. "What is your rush?"

June said, "Once he gets headed in a direction, he doesn't stop."

Lilibet knew from his past visit that that was true, but she could also see the sweet way they seemed to be in tune with each other. As they turned to leave, Dom caught June's hand, and they inched closer together as they walked to the door.

Again, the simplicity and ease of it struck her. She'd always believed love was a big, emotional thing. A feeling that plowed you over or overwhelmed you. The truth was sometimes love was warm, comfortable, easy.

She turned to Dylan. "Wanna go back upstairs?"

He shook his head. "Now that I'm up, I might as well check the overnight markets." He gave her a quick kiss. "And you might as well go upstairs and pack. I can call the pilot, and you can be out of here in an hour if you want."

She studied his handsome face. She wanted to stay. She wanted a day alone with him to bask in the glow of her newfound knowledge of love, to examine it, to enjoy it. But looking into his dark eyes, she didn't see any of what she was feeling.

She told herself she was crazy. Cuddling the night before had been too romantic to have been suggested by anyone but a guy who loved her.

Unfortunately, he'd never said it. He also had issues. Something very real might be happening between them, but he would need time to see it. Then he'd need more time to adjust to it. He might even be telling himself he didn't feel anything…or didn't want to feel anything. So, he'd need months to accept this, and she'd have to give them to him.

He might not invite her back to Belize, but he would visit her when he came to Manhattan for business and they already had dates for Thanksgiving and Christmas. Eventually, gradually, he would see they were falling in love.

Unless she was wrong?

She'd been wrong about Ben.

Maybe a little time to sort this out before they saw each other again was as much of a good thing for her as it was for him.

Not allowing herself to be offended or disappointed, she took a step back. “Yeah, I might as well go upstairs and pack.”

He headed to the office. “I’ll call the pilot.”

An hour later, he was standing at the front door, keys to his sports car in his hand. “Ready?”

She rolled her suitcase out of the elevator with her, as she walked to him. “Yeah.” She couldn’t decide if he really, really wanted to get back to work and was rushing her or if he really, really wanted to drive her to the airstrip to see her off. Her doubts doubled, but she ignored them. She wouldn’t push him. She had to let him work this out on his own or he’d never trust it. Worse, he’d run from it.

And maybe she wouldn’t trust it either. She refused to envision a future that wouldn’t happen. He actually had to share her feelings. And only he knew what those feelings were.

At the airstrip, he kissed her goodbye at the foot of the three steps into his jet. She started up the steps, turning to wave goodbye before she ducked into the airplane, but he was already headed to his car, his back to her. He hopped in without a glance in her direction and began driving toward the road.

She stood on the top step, the ocean breeze cruising over her skin, the sun warming her, the world silent, wondering if she’d imagined everything she'd thought they were feeling. Or if he'd reverted to their temporary marriage behavior.

A defense mechanism, she reminded herself.

But it didn't feel right. It was empty, cold. But sadly familiar. More familiar than the wonderful emotions they'd seemed to share the entire trip.

And that's what she needed to focus on. The truth. Not wishful thinking. Not imagining feelings that weren't there.

The sense that she'd never return to Belize tiptoed across her nerve endings.

She told herself that feeling was wrong. Eventually, Dylan would see what she did. What they had was simple. Easy. Perfect. No forced laughter or happiness. No outlandish compromises. They were attuned to each other. They fit.

Then she remembered Ben. Remembered that she might be an ace of a problem solver for other people, able to see details of their lives to help them, but she wasn't so good at seeing what was right in front of her for herself.

She boarded the plane, but after the good night's sleep she'd gotten in Dylan's arms, she didn't nap. That only served to make the flight seem longer as the positives and negatives of their situation haunted her.

He didn't call for three days, and she wouldn't let herself call him. It took that long for her to sort out her thoughts and remind herself that he had been broken. He'd experienced three big losses.

He'd protected himself with order and routines, and he would need time to adjust to any new feelings. After all, they'd been married only half of September and most of October. Almost six weeks. Enough time for her to fall in love but not enough time for him.

Still, what they had would be worth the wait.

He called on day four and told her he was coming to Manhattan for work the next day.

"Saturday?"

"It's the only day my lawyer could meet." He laughed. "He's fine with it. But Uncle Dom wants to have dinner with us tomorrow night."

The ease with which he said it erased the confusing thoughts she'd had. They were good together. Casual. Easygoing. "That's great."

"Yeah. June will be there."

"Even better." She took a soft breath, glad she could say what she was feeling. "I missed you."

"I always miss you when you leave Belize. The house seems empty and cold. And not like when we turn down the thermostat."

The memory of that night made her smile. But so did the way he thought his life empty and cold without her. It gave her the courage to say, "Then maybe we should do something about it. I could fly down to visit you on weekends. Or you could come to Manhattan more often."

"I could." He paused. "And you could come to the beach house more often."

Her heart lifted. "I could."

As if that settled it, he said, "So, dinner tomorrow night?"

"I'd love to." For the first time in their relationship, it felt like they were making a real date. As if the step they'd skipped was finally happening. And naturally, just like everything else between them.

"Don't dress up. Uncle Dom has this little Italian place he loves. Dress isn't exactly casual, but it's not fancy either."

"Okay."

"Okay." There was a smile in his voice when he said, "See you tomorrow."

Her heart sang as she disconnected the call.

CHAPTER SIXTEEN

THE FOLLOWING NIGHT, Dylan arrived at her condo door and kissed her hello before he slid her wedding ring onto her finger, taking care of that detail before they met his uncle and June. After wheeling his suitcase back to her bedroom, they left for dinner and arrived at a small Italian restaurant near Broadway with just enough space to walk between tables covered with white linen cloths. Uncle Dom waved when he saw them.

June gave them a warm smile as they reached the table. Dylan said, "It's so nice to see you again."

June accepted his hug and hugged Lilibet. Uncle Dom hugged both Dylan and Lilibet. As they sat down, the waiter walked over.

After handing out menus, he suggested they try Penne Arrabbiata, a spicy Italian dish. Dylan, Lilibet and June easily agreed, but Uncle Dom winced. "Too spicy. I'm going with chicken parmesan."

As Dylan and Dom began discussing a business venture that interested them, Dylan slid his arm along the back of her chair. She would consider it part of their ruse, except he'd done it absently, the way someone who truly liked her would do it. He'd kissed her hello. They'd nestled together in the back of the taxi. She didn't have to push him to see how good they were together. Soon he would see it himself.

Their food arrived. They oohed and aahed over the tasty dish. The hostess led arriving customers past their table to the area in the back. Others walked by as they left the busy restaurant.

But one couple stopped. "Dylan?"

Obviously surprised, Dylan rose. "Ross! It's so good to see you!"

"Meredith, this is Dylan Olsen." Ross turned to Dylan. "Dylan, this is my fiancée, Meredith."

Dylan shook her hand. "Nice to meet you, Meredith." He motioned to the table. "You remember my Uncle Dom."

Ross nodded. "I do."

"That's June." He hesitated. "And this is Lilibet. Lilibet, June, this is my friend Ross. We grew up together. Saw each other nearly every day until he went to Harvard."

Ross said, "It's nice to meet you both."

Uncle Dom said, "June is my date and Lilibet is his wife." He pointed at Dylan. "I know he hasn't been married long, but he forgets."

Dylan froze, confusing Lilibet. She expected him to explain about the quick Vegas wedding, which was why word of their marriage hadn't yet spread, but he said nothing.

Ross's eyebrows rose. "Your wife? I don't remember being invited to the wedding."

Uncle Dom snorted. "They ran away to Vegas. I wasn't invited either."

A wealth of understanding appeared in Ross's eyes. He clearly knew Dylan well, knew his story, understood how difficult the loss of his first wife had been.

Maybe he even believed like the rest of the world that Dylan would never marry again. So, his confusion made sense.

Finally, Dylan spoke. "We wanted a simple wedding."

Ross nodded. He said, "I get it," the way a long-time friend who knows the past expresses understanding. But he paused long enough that Lilibet realized he was waiting for Dylan to say more. Not a gushing expose of how he and Lilibet met or how they decided to spend the rest of their lives together. Just confirmation that he was happy. Or that he'd made a good choice.

But, again, Dylan said nothing, only stood clumsily by his chair, looking uncomfortable.

The awkwardness of the situation built. He clearly hadn't wanted her to be introduced as his wife. A few weeks ago, she wouldn't have taken that personally. But they weren't in a real relationship then. They were now.

Which made Dylan's discomfort worse. Somewhere along the line he had vowed never to remarry. Ross knew that. Yet here Dylan was, married again. Not merely married but involved with her in real life. He'd been caught in a ruse that wasn't really a ruse anymore.

It was as if he'd suddenly seen that.

And he was embarrassed.

In her heart of hearts, she knew he was more upset about someone finding out about their marriage because that would make their divorce more difficult. Except *she* wasn't embarrassed. She was happy to be with him. She would be happy if their relationship went on forever. She'd be happy to be married to him forever, not just temporarily.

But he wouldn't.

Otherwise, he wouldn't care about the divorce.

The reality of it tightened her chest.

They were not really married. Oh, they'd had the ceremony and paperwork that said they were. But it wasn't forever. It was a deal.

She wasn't really part of his life.

She was a convenience.

A hired prop.

None of this was real.

And he didn't want it to be.

The diamonds in the ring on her third finger left hand winked at her. Now, she felt as clumsy and awkward as Dylan did.

Except she was hurting. He was only embarrassed.

By the situation, she reminded herself, not her. He didn't want outsiders to know he was married. It complicated his plans.

To divorce her? Or end their relationship completely?

Ross and Meredith said all the polite things people say when they leave someone they'd run into. Dylan returned to his seat. Uncle Dom ordered dessert for everyone and decaf coffee, which made Dylan and June laugh, and everything went back to normal.

Lilibet pulled in a breath. That whole conversation had taken less than two minutes, and whatever Dylan had been feeling seemed to be gone.

But Lilibet couldn't stop the sense that that had been a reality check for her. She was happy, continually giving him the benefit of the doubt and falling in love, while he was still playing a role.

During the limo ride back to her condo, Dylan was silent. Another confirmation that the embarrassment of his friend knowing about their marriage still bothered him. While she had real feelings for him, he didn't seem to have real feelings for her. Oh, he liked her. He was certainly attracted to her. But he had not fallen in love with her, though she'd fallen in love with him.

Which had been a giant mistake. He'd told her who he was. She'd believed him. She'd seen the barriers and the defense mechanisms he'd erected to protect himself. But she'd fallen anyway, given him the benefit of the doubt—

Because he was a nice guy. But he was also stubborn. He'd been hurt by so many people that she understood the barriers he'd erected. But given how good they were together, how honest they were with each other, she'd believed those walls were coming down.

They weren't. She saw that now.

She should have protected herself. Instead, she'd been optimistic or maybe naive, and now she knew this good guy, this nice guy, didn't want anybody.

Which meant he didn't want *her*.

The pain of it mixed with her embarrassment at being so foolish.

She knew better. After Ben, she'd known to look for signs, for behaviors that indicated her partner's true feelings. Hell, Dylan had even told her he wanted nothing permanent, nothing real. And she'd still given him the benefit of the doubt.

This—no matter how much it hurt—was on her.

When they walked to her condo door, she stopped without opening it. "You know what? I'm tired."

He shrugged. "So, we'll sleep. I kind of liked our nights of cuddling in the cold."

Oh, the easy charm. How could she not fall? No matter how much it stung, she had to forgive herself for that. Even if the shame of it felt like hot lava.

"No. No cuddling tonight."

His face scrunched in confusion. "What?"

"I think our personal relationship is confusing things." She worked to sound like the professional problem solver he'd hired her to be and not a heart-broken woman who'd given him way too much of the benefit of the doubt. "I embarrassed you tonight. Did you think I wouldn't see that?"

"The *situation* embarrassed me. What am I going to tell Ross two months from now when we're divorced?"

She pulled out her key card. Pure sorrow melted her soul. Their relationship really was nothing to him. Still, a need to do her job kept her sane. "The same thing you were going to tell everybody else, I guess. Which means, if nothing else, you should have played your role tonight. Instead, you were embarrassed. Did you think your uncle didn't see that—"

"I was embarrassed by the marriage! I'm not supposed to get married again, remember? Yet one of my closest friends now knows."

He didn't have a clue. The pain of the situation told the problem solver to sit the rest of this argument out. They'd been dancing a line between their temporary marriage and real feelings, and that was the problem. What they needed was to have the conversation both of them had been avoiding.

"You know what? I do remember. You told me several times that you didn't want to get married again. Which is why it kills me that I've fallen in love with you."

His eyes narrowed, his face scrunched in confusion. "You love me?"

"And the fact that that confuses you makes me even more foolish for falling for you." She turned to the door, but frustration built inside her. Just as she'd needed to have a real conversation with her parents to end their constant nagging about her going to law school, she needed to say something now.

She faced him again. "Yes. I love you and the fact that you can't love me is killing me."

"But we talked about my past."

"Yes, we did. Then we changed. We both changed. But only I wanted to change. You didn't. You're holding on to all your past pain like a lifeline because you believe that will keep you from getting hurt. It won't. Someday you're going to wake up so damn alone, you're going to realize that protecting yourself actually hurts you worse."

She lifted her head. "And I deserve better. I deserve real love. Not romance attached to a temporary commitment. I want it all. Love, respect, romance…even disagreements and compromises." The truth of it filled her with hope. He might not be "the one," but she would get over the pain in her heart. It might take a while, but she would. But this had to be the end so she could move on.

Though her heart shattered, she said, "You know what? I'm really sorry, but I can't do this anymore. It's not working for me. You have your shares back from your uncle. Our job is done. I'll return the money for the two holidays I'm bailing on, but I need to move on and get beyond these feelings for you that I have. Feelings you don't share. I hate the way that makes me feel." She lifted her chin. "I won't be second best anymore."

She turned to go into her condo but faced him again. "And here's something good that came out of this. Next week, you can tell your uncle we had a big fight. You now have your divorce story."

With that she turned, opened her door and walked inside. She wanted to dwell on the pain of ignoring the truth that the man she'd fallen head over heels in love with would never love her back. But the thing was, she knew eventually she would be fine. She would get over this mistake—get over him—straighten up her life and have a wonderful future. It might take years, but she'd get there.

He was stuck in the past. A painful past. A past he probably reminded himself of at least once a week to keep himself from ever having real feelings again.

He would always be in his own private little hell, and she shouldn't give a damn.

But she did. He was a good guy who deserved the good life he'd never have.

While she'd never been so hurt, so alone, so empty.

And it was all her own fault. He'd told her.

Lilibet didn't sleep that night. But that didn't surprise her. She'd slept through the night with him because she'd felt safe with him. In the morning, she almost called some friends to have lunch, but he'd left his luggage. If he came back to retrieve it, she wanted to be here.

But he didn't call or come to the condo to get his things, and she realized she was wishing he would, wishing the night without her had shown him his real feelings. Obviously, it hadn't.

The emptiness of her big, totally-wrong-for-her condo closed in on her. She'd planned to spend the day contacting a real estate agent to sell her condo, but she couldn't muster the energy.

When Ben had left her, she'd needed the distraction of getting her things back to put some fight in her blood. She didn't want to fight this time.

She no longer felt foolish for not seeing Ben hadn't loved her. She no longer felt hurt or even embarrassed over his loss. Losing what she could have had with Dylan was so much worse that losing Ben had become nothing more than a distant memory.

Losing Dylan hurt her to her core. She swore it was a physical pain.

* * *

Dylan's plane landed in paradise and jarred him out of his restless sleep. He hadn't been able to contact his pilot until the wee hours of the morning and then hours had gone by before they could take off.

He was physically tired but more emotionally exhausted. He'd stared at Lilibet's door for a good twenty seconds after she'd closed it on him, numb and confused. Then he'd realized his luggage was in her bedroom.

It had seemed like the perfect excuse to knock on her door and get their marriage ruse back on track. But he'd kept thinking about the casual way she'd told him she loved him, and his heart just wanted to pull her to him and tell her he loved her too.

Because he did.

The two-minute exchange with Ross had made it clear. He hadn't been confused because one of his friends now knew he was married. What flummoxed him was that he'd *wanted* to introduce Lilibet as his wife. He'd almost been excited about it. But the feeling had brought him up short. Images had flashed in his head. Painful reminders.

And he'd panicked. Mostly because it was too soon. How could he love somebody he'd hired to play the role of his wife—

Because she was sweet and honest and funny and generous?

True. But being all those things, she deserved better than him.

She did. She really did. He was a train wreck. Her life might currently be in flux, but she had plans to fix it. And he knew she would because she was smart and loved the people she helped. She might never be a millionaire, but she'd be something he'd never really been: Happy.

He would not ruin that for her.

He'd turned from her door and pulled out his phone to call his pilot and go home, deciding that if she sent him a message to remind him of his luggage, he'd tell her he would get it on Thanksgiving.

Then he'd walked to the elevator telling himself he was fine. Because he was. He knew this life, knew how to live with disappointment. She, however, did not deserve to date him through their pretend marriage and then on December 26, wake up alone. Ending their personal relationship now was better. Fair.

He deplaned, barely noticing people scrambling around him. With no luggage to retrieve, Jeremy raced to the sedan, opened the door for him.

"Welcome home, Mr. Olsen."

He slid onto the back seat. "Thank you, Jeremy."

Jeremy closed the door and took his seat behind the car's steering wheel. For about thirty seconds, Dylan wished he'd left a sports car to drive himself home, but in the end, he was glad he'd resumed his normal routine. He might as well.

There was no sense to prolonging missing a life that couldn't be.

CHAPTER SEVENTEEN

DYLAN SPENT THE next week working harder than he had in years, but on Saturday night, he shut everything down so he could just relax. He retired to the patio after the sun set, but it seemed a waste to make a martini to drink alone, so he stretched out on a chaise lounge to listen to the ocean.

For once, it didn't soothe him. In fact, it made his loneliness more pronounced. He bounced off the chaise and started toward the beach for a walk in the dark, but his phone rang. He pulled it from his pocket and seeing his uncle's caller ID, sighed with relief.

He sank to the chaise lounge again. "Why are you calling me when you should be out with your girlfriend?"

"I saw Lilibet today."

"She's working this week." He didn't even wince at the easy lie. They'd set this up right from the beginning.

"She didn't look like she was working. Her hair was a mess. She had on sweatpants and a hoodie. I didn't even approach her when I saw her because

I knew she probably didn't want to run into anybody."

Dylan squeezed his eyes shut.

"She looked like she'd just had the worst fight of her life."

The thought of her being hurt and in pain almost did him in, but he knew this was better for her. "We did have something of a disagreement."

"About what?"

"Our understanding of our relationship seems to be shifting."

"What the hell is that supposed to mean? You're married. That's your relationship. I sure as hell hope you're not about to tell me you asked her for an open marriage."

Dylan's heart jerked at the thought of Lilibet being with another man, but he realized that's what would happen. She wouldn't pine for him forever. She would move on. By Christmas she would probably have forgotten her feelings.

It hurt to accept that, but he had to. "No open marriage, Uncle Dom. We just see some things two different ways."

"What ways?" Dom paused, but not long enough for Dylan to say anything. "She's beautiful and smart. But that didn't impress me as much as the way I'd never seen you happier. No, I take that back. Honestly, Dylan, I don't think I've ever seen you happy until I saw you with her."

"That's not true."

"Okay. You're a workaholic who loves what he does…so yeah. You've been happy with your job. But she brought something out in you. Something good. For the first time in forever, I could see you had more in your life than work."

The memory of it drifted through him. Waking happy. Her smile when she would stroll into the dining room for breakfast. How she always seemed to know the right thing to say, the right thing to wear, and always looked pretty. How she made life look so easy.

And with her it was.

"I've never yelled at you or even bossed you around, but I'm telling you right now, fix this. You need her."

"Of course I do! I'm thinking of *her*! What the hell was she thinking attaching herself to someone like me?"

Sounding surprised, Uncle Dom said, "What? Attaching herself to someone who's smart and rich and likes life?"

"I like work."

"I've seen you on the boat or enjoying a drink on your patio. You like life." Dom paused as if he'd just realized something. "That's it. That's it right there. You thought you'd marry her, and she wouldn't change you, but she did. You're happy. You like life. You don't work half as much—it scares you."

Uncle Dom had the audacity to laugh.

"Stop."

"No. For once, Dylan, I'm going to butt in."

"For once? You always butt in!"

"No. I don't—not on the big things—and I should have. I should have told you Janine was all wrong for you."

The truth of that made him feel like he was suffocating. He'd known it, deep down. But he'd been so bowled over by her that he couldn't believe it wasn't right.

"Then life did you dirty with the way she was taken. It would have been enough to jar anyone, but your marriage also sucked and you blamed yourself for an accident."

He had. But it was a truth he couldn't avoid.

"You can't blame yourself for an accident. The bad marriage yes. But not the accident."

"I ruined the last years of her life."

"She could have just as easily divorced you. She chose to stay."

"So did I."

"So what? She also made the choice to stay. And you've punished yourself enough, because now there's a person in your life who makes you happy and you're hurting her because you think you still deserve to be punished. You don't. But punishing yourself is safe, easy. It's what you know how to do. Being in a good relationship is new for you, and you know better than anyone there are no guarantees. But that woman loves you and you love her. It's like life is giving you a second chance. Not everybody gets that."

Dylan sat perfectly still. He never thought about things like second chances. There had been no such thing as a second chance when his dad died or when Janine was killed or when his mom left. All he ever saw in life were endings.

But what if this was a beginning? He could almost see his life with Lilibet unfolding with happiness. Maybe kids? Maybe a new house in New England? Christmases with snow in the winter. Then teaching their kids to water ski and drive the boat in Belize. Actually having that honeymoon in Paris.

His heart gave his brain permission to hope.

But it wouldn't happen naturally, and he knew he was at a crossroad. Was he a coward or a dreamer? Someone who grabbed on to hope with both hands and let him take it where it would. He'd never expected a second chance. He'd never even considered it. Considering it now brought up bad memories, reminded him that being vulnerable usually meant being hurt.

But it also meant a better life.

And he knew the truth.

He either faced this or he lost her. He would lose the smart, easygoing, talented, open, wonderful woman who loved him.

Loved him.

He knew Lilibet didn't feel anything lightly.

Her honesty wouldn't let her. If she said she loved him, she meant it with her whole heart and soul.

Did he really want to walk away from that?

Lose real love?

Early Sunday morning, Lilibet was walking up her hallway to get coffee, when she heard the doorbell, then an impatient knock. She blew her breath out on a long sigh and prayed it wasn't her mom. She wasn't in the mood to pretend she was happy.

Just to be on the safe side, she looked through her peephole and saw Dylan. Not in the suit and tie he typically wore for business trips, in jeans and a sweatshirt.

Her heart quivered. She really didn't want to see him. She'd envisioned a hazy, but happy future for them. She'd given him the benefit of the doubt. She'd *worried* about him. But she hadn't had any impact on him. Except that she played her role as wife very well.

Of course, she'd told him she would reimburse the part of the fee he'd paid her for Thanksgiving and Christmas dinners with his uncle. Maybe he wanted to talk about that.

She shook her head. Even if that was true, he could email her. She did not want to see him.

He rang the bell again.

Then she remembered she had his luggage.

She had to see him.

Deciding to get everything over with at once,

she raced back to her room to get the wedding ring she'd forgotten to give him the week before. Then raced up the hall again and yanked open the door.

He didn't even wait for her to say hello before he blurted, "I do love you and that scared me to death."

She blinked. "What?"

He loved her?

Her breathing stopped. She'd longed to hear him say that, but she also knew what a big deal it was for him. He must have spent the week soul-searching.

And realized what she'd been seeing. They loved each other.

But was that enough?

Was it even real or just the loneliness of living in a big house with no one but staff to keep him company?

"I haven't trusted anyone in four years. I check out my business partners every time they make a move. I'm still wary of June Bug. But you? I feel like I could hand you my soul and you'd take care of it."

The poetry of it opened her heart. For as much as she'd like to kick his butt for the suffering she'd endured in the past week, she couldn't. Life had brutalized him. And he had probably struggled to come to terms with this.

Not merely to come to terms with it but flying

to Manhattan and telling her. That meant something.

Hope built in her soul. She wasn't jumping to conclusions, but she wouldn't hinder him either.

"Yes. I would take care of your soul."

"We've only known each other a few weeks."

Tears filled her eyes as she smiled. "Technically, we've known each other for years. We simply haven't seen each other. And we're married."

A move of her hand displayed the ring they'd made their vows with. Today, it didn't demonstrate the ruse. It didn't remind him that it was part of a plan. Today, it looked to be exactly where it was supposed to be.

It should have elevated his fear. Instead, an unexpected joy filled him. "Our time together has been the weirdest thing."

"I've said that all along."

He took a step toward her. "Come here."

She hesitated, so he breached the distance between them, holding on to her for dear life. "I am so sorry that it took me so long to realize life was giving me a second chance." He stepped back so he could loosen his hold and look into her eyes. "A wonderful second chance. You are happy and fun. Yet you can be serious and logical. You love my crazy uncle. You were always good to him and June. And you were good to me. You could have played our marriage so differently, but you showed my uncle your good, happy side. And I saw it, too."

She straightened defensively. "I'm a good, happy person. I wasn't acting."

"I think that's the point. I've never met anybody like you. In fact, if I'd paid closer attention to you when I first met you at the pub all those years ago, I could have saved myself a lot of pain and suffering. You were right there in front of me…the right person to marry…the right person to love, but I thought I knew better."

She laughed. "You always think you know better. And sometimes you do. That's what makes life confusing."

He laughed.

She stepped close to him again. "Now, kiss me and make this official."

He obliged, pulling her tight against him as his lips met hers in happy connection. Fears he'd had for years melted away. The confusion he'd always carried about relationships disappeared too. She would never leave him, never hurt him… She'd argue with him. She'd make him see the right thing to do and offer valuable opinions. But she would never hurt him.

Because they were partners. Good for each other. They fit.

He saw that now.

Thank God.

EPILOGUE

SIX MONTHS LATER, they stood in a reception line for the big wedding celebration that Uncle Dom wanted. Unable to find her original wedding dress in the charity shop where she'd donated it, Lilibet had purchased a new one. It wasn't exactly like the one Dylan had bought, but it was close enough that she believed she looked as she had when she'd married him.

As one wedding guest walked away and another took the few steps to replace them, he bent to kiss her. "You look amazing."

She laughed. "I was trying very hard to duplicate our wedding, but I couldn't find the dress."

"Doesn't matter. You look beautiful." He caught her gaze. "You are beautiful."

She laughed.

"Besides you have the ring. That's what matters."

She glanced down at it lovingly. "I do. When you first gave it to me, it felt big and awkward. Now, it just feels like an anchor. Or a guiding light."

"That's because it's where it belongs."

Ross and Meredith walked up to them. Ross reached for Dylan's hand to shake it. "Congratulations."

Dylan shook Ross's hand then hugged Meredith who also said, "Congratulations."

"We're so glad you could come," Lilibet said as she hugged Meredith.

Ross said, "I have to admit we were surprised by the invitation."

Lilibet rolled her eyes. "We got married in Vegas the first time and Uncle Dom felt cheated. He wanted a party."

Ross laughed. "He does like a good party." He clapped Dylan's shoulder. "It's nice to see you happy again. And I think Uncle Dom's glad he doesn't have to watch over you anymore."

Dylan snorted. "Now, it's me watching over him."

Ross said, "Yeah. I see he's still with the woman he was with when we saw you at the restaurant. Very un-Uncle-Dom-like."

Dylan laughed. "He's giving real romance a chance."

"Well, this should be fun."

They all laughed, then Ross and Meredith entered the ballroom and Dylan and Lilibet accepted congratulations from the four hundred guests

Uncle Dom and her parents had insisted on, but she'd never been happier.

She had Dylan now. A man who loved her for exactly who she was. That was all she needed.

* * * * *

If you enjoyed this story, check out these other great reads from Susan Meier

Secret Fling with the King
One-Night Baby with the Best Man
Mother of the Bride's Second Chance
It Started with a Proposal

All available now!